Annie froze as he moved one hand, his palm cupping her cheek, the caress of his fingers sending a trail of heat across her skin and firing every nerve-ending to zinging awareness.

His thumb under her chin tilted her face up until she could no longer avoid his gaze.

'How is it possible that you are even more beautiful than ever?'

His husky words sent waves of arousal washing through her, tightening her insides and speeding her pulse. Every part of her was on red alert, his touch, his nearness, his musky male scent all combining to rob her of common sense and strip away her resistance.

'Nathan...'

Her warning stalled, his name escaping on a whisper of breath rather than sounding like the denial she had intended. And when the pad of his thumb grazed across the swell of her lower lip she couldn't maintain coherent thought. Instead, her traitorous lips parted in eager anticipation when his own brushed across them. She responded instinctively as his mouth captured hers, demanding, needy, plunging her back into the once familiar abyss of heady excitement and unquenchable desire.

Annie had forgotten how incredible Nathan's seductive, erotic kisses were. No, that was wrong. She hadn't forgotten...

Dear Reader

I was starting to write Nathan and Annie's story when I was invited to take part in some special projects to celebrate Mills & Boon's centenary in 2008.

Nathan was left pacing restlessly in my mind, demanding I get down to the business of reuniting him with Annie, his heroine, who has appeared as a secondary character in several of my previous Medicals™. But Annie doesn't want a reunion with the man she once loved beyond reason—the man she thinks rejected her five years ago.

Now Nathan and Annie must work together as dedicated A&E doctors. Although Annie tries to keep Nathan at bay, she is forced to confront the past and her role in it, discovering that her reality is distorted. As the truth becomes clear, Annie's plans backfire on her—and then an event threatens to change her life for ever. Is it too late for them, or can Nathan and Annie have a second chance at love?

It is wonderful to be back in my fictional world of Strathlochan again, catching up with old friends and making new ones. I hope you will enjoy Nathan and Annie's story...and return to visit the folk in Strathlochan again very soon.

Love

Margaret

www.margaretmcdonagh.com

THE EMERGENCY DOCTOR CLAIMS HIS WIFE

BY
MARGARET McDONAGH

MILLS & BOON®
Pure reading pleasure™

First published in Great Britain 2009
Harlequin Mills & Boon Limited,
Eton House, 18-24 Paradise Road, Richmond, Surrey TW9 1SR

© Margaret McDonagh 2009

ISBN: 978 0 263 20919 8

Set in Times R
15-0309-53008

Printed and bou
by CPI Antony

Margaret McDonagh says of herself: 'I began losing myself in the magical world of books from a very young age, and I always knew that I had to write, pursuing the dream for over twenty years, often with cussed stubbornness in the face of rejection letters! Despite having numerous romance novellas, short stories and serials published, the news that my first "proper book" had been accepted by Harlequin Mills & Boon for their Medical™ Romance line brought indescribable joy! Having a passion for learning makes researching an involving pleasure, and I love developing new characters, getting to know them, setting them challenges to overcome. The hardest part is saying goodbye to them, because they become so real to me. And I always fall in love with my heroes! Writing and reading books, keeping in touch with friends, watching sport and meeting the demands of my four-legged companions keeps me well occupied. I hope you enjoy reading this book as much as I loved writing it.'

www.margaretmcdonagh.com
margaret.mcdonagh@yahoo.co.uk

Praise for Medical™ Romance author Margaret McDonagh:

'This is such a beautiful, wonderfully told and poignant story that I truly didn't want it to end. Margaret McDonagh is an exceptional writer of romantic fiction, and with VIRGIN MIDWIFE, PLAYBOY DOCTOR she will tug at your heartstrings, make you cry, and leave you breathless!'
—*The Pink Heart Society Reviews*

'Romance does not get any better than this! Margaret McDonagh is a writer readers can always count on to deliver a story that's poignant, emotional and spellbinding, and AN ITALIAN AFFAIR is no exception!'
—*CataRomance.com*

To Christina Jones and Maggie Kingsley
—my deadline buddies—
thank you for all the support and encouragement

And to Dr Nick Edwards—thanks for your help
and for your wonderful book, *In Stitches*,
which is funny, moving and thought-provoking

CHAPTER ONE

'HAVE you seen him yet, Annie?'

Dr Annie Webster glanced round in response to the question and stifled a groan at the hungry anticipation on Olivia Barr's heavily made-up face. The trauma nurse—famous for her short attention span and her even shorter skirts—was staring out of the ground floor staffroom window which overlooked the car park outside the casualty department at Strathlochan Hospital. Accustomed to her ways, the handful of other staff present paid Olivia no mind.

'Seen who?' Annie queried, feigning interest as she poured herself a fortifying cup of coffee which she just had time to savour before her shift in A and E began.

'The new doctor. He started yesterday. But you were off then, weren't you?' Thickly kohled brown eyes glittered as Olivia assessed her for a moment before dismissing her. She teased artfully placed strands of short, bleached blonde hair across her forehead and resumed her watch from the window. 'Here comes his car now. Oh, yes! Talk about sexy. Wait until you see the body on this man!'

Annie expected the woman to start drooling any moment. As one of the other nurses nearby rolled her eyes behind Olivia's back, Annie stifled a laugh. Olivia's reputation as a man eater was well earned, and she went after anyone who took her fancy with frightening zest. Olivia might have her moments as a good trauma nurse, but Annie disapproved of her obvious, often embarrassing crushes on male visitors and colleagues. Fortunately for all concerned these never lasted long—her interest rarely being reciprocated—before she moved on to the next man to catch her eye. Unfortunately these distractions often affected her concentration and, worst of all, her patient care—something Annie could not ignore or forgive.

'I've found out he's not married but I know precious little else about him…yet.' Olivia's scarlet-painted mouth set in an unattractive sulky moue of displeasure. 'So far he's been difficult to pin down and has refused to answer my questions.'

Annie didn't blame the guy. Clearly this new doctor had his wits about him if he had summed Olivia up on day one and managed to maintain his distance. The woman was nothing if not persistent in pursuit of what she wanted.

'I don't plan to let this one slip through my fingers. He's something else.' Olivia rubbed her hands together, looking for all the world like a predator in pursuit of its prey and preparing an imminent ambush.

Shaking her head, Annie cupped her coffee mug, warming her hands as she crossed the room, curiosity drawing her to peep out of the window to see the new man who was the latest to capture Olivia's attention. It was a cold, grey January day, and a misty drizzle coated the landscape. Low cloud blocked out the hills and the view of the loch in the valley below, around two banks of which the expanding town of Strathlochan sprawled. Although there had been much less snow than last winter, frosty nights were following wet days and the subsequent icy conditions kept the A and E department busy, dealing with injuries from both road accidents and fallen pedestrians.

Annie's attention returned to the car outside as a blatantly male figure emerged. An inexplicable shiver of unease tingled down her spine. The man had his back to them as he locked the driver's door, his athletically muscled frame encased in jeans and a well-worn leather jacket. As he walked towards the building with a loose-limbed stride, his warm breath vapourising in the frigid air, the wind teased his dark hair and he turned his head, raising a hand to brush the wayward strands back from his face, giving Annie her first proper glimpse of him.

Shocked, she stepped back from the window, struggling to contain her horrified gasp as recognition slammed into her. The disturbingly familiar body and the patrician profile were unforgettable.

For a breathless moment Annie was sure she had to be hallucinating. A tremor rippled through her. No! No way could Nathan Shepherd be here. Not at her hospital. It was a trick of the light or some unaccountable blip in her imagination. It wasn't true. Nathan was *not* in Strathlochan.

Trying to steady her breathing and ignore the way her heart was thudding wildly in her chest, she turned away, deaf to Olivia's excited appraisal and the chatty greetings as more staff arrived for their shifts.

With shaky fingers Annie set down her still-full mug, her need for caffeine forgotten, and left the staffroom. She walked partway down the corridor and stopped to peer round the corner. The transparent Plexiglas panels in the rubber swing doors leading to the busy A and E department allowed her a better view of the man who now stood at the reception counter.

There was no mistaking that strong, handsome face and

sexy body. Nathan *was* in Strathlochan. And, judging by
the way he was looking over a set of notes and giving
advice to one of the nurses, and the official ID tag hanging
around his neck, it was true he was here to work. In her
department! Hell and damnation. Every part of her quiver-
ing with shock and alarm, Annie leaned against the wall,
her breath locked in her throat, her fingers clenched into
fists at her sides. What was she going to do?

'Annie, are you all right?' An older nurse, in the process
of bringing a patient in a wheelchair back from the radiology department, if the large envelope containing X-ray
images was any guide, paused at the swing doors.

'Sorry?' Annie blinked, focusing on the matronly woman's
concerned face. 'Um, yes. I'm fine, Gail.' She flinched at the
lie, knowing she was anything but fine. 'Thanks.'

Gail smiled and nodded towards the bustling reception
area. 'Quite something, isn't he?'

'I beg your pardon?'

'Our new doctor. Nathan Shepherd. He's taken over
while Trevor Wilkinson is on long-term sick leave. Started
yesterday. He's quite reserved but an excellent doctor. And
very easy on the eyes! He made a real impact with both
staff and patients. Especially Olivia…but that doesn't
surprise anyone!' Gail grinned conspiratorially before
pushing through the doors and wheeling her charge
towards the plaster room.

The sound of Gail's footsteps and the noisy hum of the
department receded as the doors closed, but it took Annie
a moment to move. Oh, God! Battling a fresh wave of
shock, she hurried to the ladies' restroom, went into a
cubicle and shut the door, needing privacy. In a daze, she
sat down. This wasn't a dream from which she was about
to wake up. It was a nightmare. And far, far too real.

'No! No, no, no…' Annie bent forward and buried her face in her hands. 'This cannot be happening. How can fate be so cruel?'

Nathan was here and she was going to have to see him, talk to him, work with him. Sitting back, she closed her eyes and pressed the heel of one hand to the pain that now gripped her chest. Nathan Shepherd. The man she had expected to marry. The man she had determined would be the father of her children. The man she had loved more than she had imagined it was possible to love anyone. The man who had rejected her and broken her heart five years ago.

Now he had reappeared unexpectedly in her life, and one brief sight of him gave the lie to any belief that she had forgotten about him—had recovered from him. One look had brought back all the pain, all the love, all the hurt, all the memories. It was as if the years had been stripped away and every feeling, every nerve-ending, was exposed and raw again. She realised with sick despair that there had been nothing but a temporary sticking plaster masking her wounds, lulling her into a false sense of security. In one unguarded moment the covering had been cruelly ripped off to reveal how little she had healed, leaving her open, hurting, vulnerable.

Nathan's arrival in Strathlochan was a disaster of un-imaginable proportions. Annie wrapped her arms around her midriff, seeking comfort as wave after wave of memories washed over her in an unstoppable tide. When she heard the outer door open, to admit a couple of laughing women, she clamped one hand over her mouth to stifle the moan of anguish her recollections had produced.

Nathan…

Shaking, she sat in silence, anxious not to be discovered, breathing a sigh of relief as the two women shut off the water taps, finished whatever they were doing and left the cloakroom. The door closed on more of their carefree laughter. Annie doubted she would ever feel so light-hearted again.

The hours of her shift stretched ahead like the worst kind of punishment, and she wished she could hide out in this cubicle until it was time to go home. But she couldn't shirk her responsibilities. Patients needed her. Colleagues depended on her. She wouldn't let them down. And she could not allow Nathan's presence in the department to turn her back into the broken person she had been when she had arrived in Strathlochan after their break-up. A break-up that had followed just a few months after the sudden and un-expected death of her beloved father, when she had already been so vulnerable. She was stronger now—more confi-dent, more mature, successful in her career. It had been a hard slog, but she had done it. Whatever it cost her, Nathan would not take that progress away from her as he had taken away her dreams.

Knowing that someone else could come into the restroom at any moment, Annie forced herself to move. Her heart thudded against her ribs as she left the cubicle and checked her appearance in the mirror. She was determined to maintain a cool façade, despite the nerves that were tangling inside her, making her feel sick and unsteady. But Nathan would never know what seeing him again did to her. Somehow she would survive this shift, and then she would decide what to do. For once she gave thanks for Olivia's excesses. The nurse had unwittingly alerted her to Nathan's presence, giving her some time to prepare. Better this than the shock of coming face to face with him without prior warning.

Glancing at her watch, she groaned. It was time for the

shift hand-over. Unable to linger indefinitely, she sucked in a deep, steadying breath, raised her chin in defiance, then opened the door and walked down the short corridor to confront her past.

Despite her good intentions, her steps faltered when she spotted Nathan on the far side of the group of staff gathered around senior consultant Robert Mowbray. Nathan had changed into the customary green scrubs worn by doctors in the department. A stethoscope was looped around his neck over his photo ID badge, drawing attention to his strong shoulders and broad chest. Thankful to hang back, sheltered from Nathan's view by a crush of other colleagues, Annie endeavoured to concentrate as members of the previous shift detailed the patients still being cared for within the department.

Unsettled, she adjusted her position until she was able to observe Nathan without him being aware of her. Her chest tightened and her heart gave an irregular and worrisome flip as she assessed her former lover, taking in his familiar stance and the intentness of his expression as he jotted down some notes. She was unsurprised by his thoroughness. Nathan had always been dedicated to patient care. It was one of the many things she had admired... loved...about him. The pain inside her intensified. Her traitorous gaze drank him in, as if needing to quench an endless and long-endured thirst.

His dark brown hair was as rakish as ever—untamed and in need of a cut. She remembered what it had been like to sink her fingers into that hair, could almost feel again the luxuriant silken thickness of it against her skin. As she watched, he raised a hand and absently brushed a fallen lock back from his brow. Strong, capable hands. Hands that could heal. Hands that could bring unimaginable pleasure.

Another shiver rippled through her as she remembered the caress of those hands on her body, the brush and stroke of those clever fingers over super-sensitive skin.

She remembered, too, how slumberous dark eyes framed by impossibly long lashes had turned almost black with hot passion when he'd made love to her. And, oh, *how* he had made love to her! Intensely, wickedly, gloriously, end-lessly…with generosity, fire, sinful inventiveness and a single-minded dedication to meet her every need and leave her boneless, breathless and deliciously satisfied. Every feminine part of her tightened, a desperate ache of want lodging deep inside her. She closed her eyes, trying to fight back the erotic memories. But it didn't help. They were impinged on her brain for ever, and even five years of sep-aration and determined efforts to forget him had not worked.

Nathan was the same, yet different. He had always been impressive to look at, but the past years had seen his six-foot-two-inch body harden and mature even more, while his face appeared leaner, more angular, but just as devas-tatingly arresting. He had a presence, a latent sexuality that was impossible to ignore, and he was way too handsome and compelling for her peace of mind. Yet he had also been quiet and reserved, mysterious, unapproachable, allowing few people close enough to glimpse the real man hidden inside. A caring man, dedicated to his job, serious and watchful, with a smile all the more heart-stopping for its recipient because of its rarity. At least that was how she had felt. And at one time those special smiles and all that intensity had been for her and her alone—until the fateful moment it had all blown up in her face and their relation-ship had been over.

Smarting with fresh pain, Annie wondered how Nathan would feel when he discovered she was here. Thankfully, she had the advantage of knowing what was to come. Would he be as shocked and disturbed as she had been at her first sight of him? Would his body feel the unwanted yet instinctive reaction to her presence as hers did to his? Would he feel anything after five years? He'd rejected her, after all.

She had no more time to ponder on her questions as the consultant chose that moment to dismiss the group and her musings were curtailed. He looked up, saw her, and beckoned for her to join him.

'Annie, could you stay back a moment, please?' Robert Mowbray requested, earning her a fulminating, envious glare from Olivia as the nurse flounced away.

As the other staff dispersed, to tend to their assigned patients and assist the new ones arriving all the time, Annie fought a fresh welling of panic and reluctantly walked forward. If she had been in trouble before, meeting Nathan's dark gaze set off an internal earthquake, way off the Richter scale, rocking her to her foundations. She felt weak, shaken, challenged. Immediately she realised she did not have the upper hand at all. Nathan looked far from surprised to see her. He watched her, silent, unreadable, in control. A barely there, secret smile tipped one corner of his sensual mouth, stirring her blood, tangling her nerves into knots and making her feel in imminent danger of losing her senses. Deliberately she looked away and focused on Robert, desperate for something—anything— to ground her back in reality.

'Nathan, this is Dr Annie Webster—one of our specialist registrars.' As the consultant, short, stocky and approaching retirement age, introduced them, Annie was relieved that he appeared unaware of any past history between Nathan and herself. 'Annie, meet our new Senior House Officer, Nathan Shepherd.'

Surprise held her silent for several moments. Surprise because, whatever else had passed between them on a personal level, she knew that Nathan was an amazing doctor. Not only was he academically brilliant—she had achieved far more in medical school thanks to Nathan's help with her studies than she ever would have alone—but he was also someone who had a natural empathy with patients. They trusted him and, however awkward and aloof he seemed in social settings, he had an innate ability to set those in his care at ease.

Knowing he was a vastly better doctor than she could ever hope to be, he should be way ahead of her in qualifications by now. Especially as he had been so focused, so dedicated. Wasn't that why he had not wanted to commit to her or to their relationship? It didn't make sense that she had recently achieved her specialist registrar status while he was still an SHO. Why? What had happened to hold him back? Not that it was any of her business. She didn't want to know, she assured herself. But still…

A discreet cough from Robert Mowbray brought her mind back to the present uncomfortable situation. 'Annie?'

'Yes.' She battled to maintain her composure. 'I remember Dr Shepherd. We knew of each other some years ago, when we were training.'

Proud of herself for remaining outwardly calm, she smiled politely as she extended her hand for a swift shake, hastily withdrawing it before the full force of the electric current that zapped along her nerve-endings could reduce her to mush. *Damn it.* She had hoped to feel nothing. Far from it. Every atom of her being was alive with sensation.

'Annie.'

Just one word, delivered in that no-nonsense Lancastrian voice, rough-edged and seductive in tone, shook her to the core—again—overloading her with memories. Memories of long hours of loving, of Nathan's constant support and encouragement, of the way he had helped her study, keeping her supplied with her favourite apple and toffee doughnuts from the local bakery, of the private Nathan, relaxed and laughing…and of the searing pain of their furious parting.

Her gaze flicked to Nathan's, then skittered away in alarm. She knew she had to say something, to respond in welcome, but… Behind her back she knotted her hands together, then drew in a lungful of air, trying to centre herself. She could do this. She could pretend his presence here didn't matter, that he didn't affect her as she apparently didn't affect him.

'How pleasant to see you again, Nathan. It's good of you to step in like this and help out on a temporary basis.'

Pleasant? Temporary? They had known each other when they were training?

A muscle pulsed along Nathan's jaw as he fought to keep his emotions in check. Annie could dismiss all they had once shared with those coolly formal words? He hadn't been sure what to expect when they met again, and he had been glad to have yesterday to settle in, acquaint himself with his new colleagues and learn the lie of the land at the hospital before coming face to face with Annie. The department had been busy, the work varied and involving, and if he hadn't been so gut-wrenchingly nervous about seeing Annie some time soon he would have enjoyed himself. As much as he had enjoyed anything without her in his life.

Since deciding to take this post in Strathlochan he had spent a ridiculous amount of time wondering what Annie would say and do, how it would feel to see her again, if she would be welcoming or displeased to see him. Now it was clear she was neither. Apparently she felt nothing at all—and her casual indifference hurt more than anything. She was treating him like some barely remembered inconsequential acquaintance, rather than the lover she had professed to adore beyond reason.

Their row that last dreadful day, and the way she had left him, had broken his heart, destroyed the hopes and dreams he had dared to believe in since meeting her. Now he looked at her, stunned at the dismissive uninterest in those amazing blue eyes. He might not have expected her to greet him with open arms—had even anticipated a few moments of characteristic temper and stubbornness—but he hadn't been prepared for her cool unconcern.

The pain in his gut intensified. He had thought she might have grown up in five years, hoped she would have mellowed, matured, reasoned things out…understood that he hadn't been the bad guy. She had been the one to end it, after all—to throw away everything they had on a whim, indulging in a customary tantrum because she hadn't got her own way. But clearly Annie had not changed. Old hurts and the smart of injustice fired anew within him.

Practised at hiding his inner feelings, he took a few moments to study her. It was hardly possible, but she looked even more beautiful than ever—as if she had grown into herself during the intervening years. Above average height, her slender figure had a feminine lushness, firing his erotic fantasies, and the shapeless green scrubs hid a body he knew as intimately as his own. A body that was all woman, with long, toned limbs and mouthwatering curves. He knew every hollow, every freckle, every dip and rise, knew the silky-soft feel of her skin, the honey-sweet taste of her, knew her sensuous jasmine fragrance. Knew, too, just where to touch, kiss, lick and suck to keep her on the brink, before shooting her into the stratosphere with pleasure. And he knew the sounds she made achieving the peak of ecstasy.

Her skin was creamy and translucent, her eyes a rich, dark blue, and her ebony hair was as glossy but shorter than it had been, now brushing her shoulders in tousled waves. She didn't look a day older, but there was a new poise and confidence about her, a new drive and ambition. He'd heard how respected she was in the department, what a good doctor she had become. He was proud of her and her achievements, the way she had fast attained her specialist registrar status, but he also knew a moment of surprise that she now appeared the single-minded career woman. Annie had always been caring and warm, dedicated to her patients, but she had been carefree and impish too—quirky, with a zest for living, desperate to combine being a doctor with having fun...and a family of her own.

How much of that side of her remained? he wondered now, watching her unsmiling face, her shuttered expression, trying to banish the rush of mixed emotions that seeing her again had evoked in him. Not because he hadn't expected it—she was why he was here, after all—but because of her response to him. Or her lack of one. Annie seemed not to care a damn about his sudden presence in Strathlochan.

'I hope you enjoy your stay with us, Nathan,' she murmured, her voice cool, more refined, yet still carrying a recognisable thread of her Yorkshire upbringing.

Scared his plans were going to hell in a handcart, he somehow managed a polite nod and kept his own voice composed. 'Thank you.' He needed to regroup, to re-evaluate his mission here.

'The fact that you are old friends makes my decision an easy one.' Robert Mowbray's words drew Nathan's attention, and he turned to face the older man. 'Annie, I want you to be Nathan's support while he settles in here,' the consultant continued, apparently unaware of the tension crackling around them. 'I'll make sure your shifts are scheduled together for the time being.'

Nathan heard Annie's indrawn hiss of breath, and when he glanced at her he saw the momentary spark of horrified panic in her eyes. Maybe she wasn't as calm and unaffected as she wanted him to think. Interesting.

'Nathan's reputation as a trauma doctor precedes him, and I worked alongside him yesterday so I know his skills first-hand. He won't need babysitting, Annie, but the plan is for him to make up to specialist registrar grade while he's here. We'll do all we can to ensure that happens. Were it not for his time outside a hospital environment he would be well ahead of you on the career ladder.'

Nathan frowned. He would sooner Robert Mowbray kept any additional details to himself. Another glance at Annie revealed a spark of curiosity flickering in her eyes— one he had not expected to see. In all their time together they had been as physically intimate as it was possible to be, but she had never shown any deeper interest in his background, for which he had been relieved and thankful. The fact that Annie had never asked questions, that she'd been so open and had lived only for the moment, had been amongst the many things that had drawn him to her in the first place. She'd been different from anyone he had ever known, a refreshing change after his dour home-life laden with problems, disappointments and the heavy weight of unwanted responsibility.

He was jolted from his thoughts as a nurse bustled up

to them. Matronly, with greying hair and smiling hazel
eyes, Nathan remembered her name was Gail.

'Excuse me interrupting, but we have two ambulances
on the way in,' she informed them. 'There was a collision in town. It's believed an elderly woman had a heart
attack at the wheel. Her car mounted the pavement and
hit a gentleman shopper. He is reported to have multiple
leg fractures. Both were said to be serious but stable at
the scene.'

Robert snapped to attention. 'Right. Thank you, Gail.
I'll take the woman with heart problems. Annie, you and
Nathan attend to the man with fractures. Gail, ask the on-
call radiographer to come down, please. And we'll need
people from both Cardiology and Orthopaedics.'

As Gail hurried off to carry out her duties, Robert went
into a resus bay to organise his team. Nathan followed
Annie into another. Pulling on a lead apron with "Team
Leader" written on the back, she briefed the staff who had
gathered, each of whom were donning their own lead
aprons as well as gloves and eye protection—standard
safety devices used in the department.

'Nathan will be designated Doctor 1 and Gus Doctor 2,'
she clarified, checking to see that the nurses were set and
that the room was prepared for the patient's arrival. 'Holly
will work with Nathan, Gail with Gus, and Carolyn will act
as scribe and complete the Trauma Sheet. The anaesthetist
is here, and a radiographer is on the way. Everyone ready?'

A chorus of agreement greeted her question as each
member of staff set about their appointed tasks. Noting that
junior doctor Gus Buchanan was seeing to the blood bottles
and forms, Gail was preparing warm fluids, and Holly was
phoning the lab and writing up details on the white board
on the wall, Nathan headed out with Annie towards the

outer doors of the casualty department, where they joined
the wait for the ambulances with Robert and his head nurse.

The familiar charge of adrenalin hit him. He remained
painfully aware of Annie's presence, and her antipathy,
but he had to try and force thoughts of her out of his mind
for the moment. It wasn't easy, however. She had haunted
his every waking moment and his every dream at night for
five long years—ever since the moment she had shattered
his heart and his reason for being.

The silence, the loneliness, the darkness of his time
without her had cut deep. He had loved her…truly, deeply,
completely. She had brought fun and sunshine into his otherwise grey, joyless life. A life that had returned to being
colourless and dull without her effervescent presence and
the warmth of her love. The light had gone when she had
left him and had never returned. Now with the other responsibilities that had burdened his life for so long in some
kind of order, he had needed to find Annie again, to bring
closure to a part of his life that felt unfinished.

Part of him had hoped he would see Annie and feel
nothing—that the love would have gone and he would be
set free, released from the prison he'd been in for five
years. A prison in which he had been in solitary confine-
ment and to which only Annie held the key to release him.
Then perhaps he could put the past behind and move on
with his life without Annie haunting him. But it wasn't to
be. The second he had seen her again he had known with
a mix of excitement and despair that the love and desire
was still there and the craving had not gone away. Being
near her again was overwhelming his senses. Annie still
held his emotions in a stranglehold.

It would be far better for him if he did feel nothing. Yet
one look and he knew he still cared for her with everything

in him. Despite what she had done, despite the hurt she had caused him running away as she had, he still wanted her, needed her, loved her. Which made his life horribly complicated and uncertain. Given her reception of him, the chance that they could reconcile the past, let alone re-establish any kind of relationship, was seeming less and less likely. Once again he was opening himself up to inevitable heartbreak and rejection, and he wasn't sure he could survive that a second time.

The sound of sirens drew him from his troubled thoughts, and he watched the flashing blue lights of the two ambulances come closer as they moved up the hill through the lingering mist and turned in at the hospital entrance. As the first backed into the bay, Robert moved forward to hurry the elderly woman through to Resus.

When the back doors of the second ambulance opened moments later, Nathan and Annie helped the paramedics manoeuvre the stretcher out, ready to speed the badly injured patient inside. One of the paramedics was keeping pressure on an open wound in the man's right thigh, temporarily stemming what Nathan could see was a bad bleed.

As Annie led the way to Resus, she looked at him, and he recognised in her the same charge of adrenalin and call to duty that sang in his own veins. Then her dark blue eyes narrowed briefly, and her voice was cool and professional.

'Right, Nathan, let's see how good a doctor you still are.'

'Be careful issuing challenges, Annie,' he murmured, keeping his voice low, so no one else could hear, seeing the surprise and alarm on her face as she hesitated. 'In the days and weeks ahead I plan to show you what you walked away from and what you are missing out on. And I'm not just talking about my medical skills.'

Aware he had shaken her, he left Annie to mull over his

words. Snapping back into professional mode as the paramedics wheeled the stretcher inside the designated resus bay, and the patient was transferred to the trolley bed, his focus was now solely on the man who needed the team's attention and medical know-how.

Dealing with Annie—and confronting their past—would have to wait a little longer.

CHAPTER TWO

ANNIE was shaking as she followed Nathan inside Resus Bay Two. If only she hadn't been foolish enough to issue that meaningless challenge. Now she fretted over his words, worried about what he had meant. Surely he didn't think there could be anything left between them? Anxiety tightened inside her, and she cursed herself for allowing him to fluster her, derail her. The last thing she needed was to have to work closely with Nathan in the days ahead.

'This is Len Gordon. Age fifty-nine. Multiple lower limb fractures, plus femoral break and bleed. Query possible damage to his pelvis. He's in shock and his blood pressure is low.'

Annie forced herself to set her private concerns aside, and listened as the paramedics finished their report on the patient's condition, running through GCS score, level of consciousness at the scene and since, BP, respiration, pulse rate and oxygen saturation, plus details of the fluids and drugs already given. Her job as Team Leader was to co-ordinate rather than be hands-on, so she stood back and watched as the trauma team swung smoothly into action, each focusing on their individual role yet combining as one unit. Once the initial examination had been made, she would be called upon to make decisions about what to do next.

The department's resus teams were well prepared, and the best Annie had worked with. While the anaesthetic nurse was calming and reassuring the patient, getting what details she could from the distressed, confused man and keeping him informed about what was going on, the anaesthetist concentrated on securing Len's airway, breathing and circulation.

Annie checked the ECG and vital function monitors one of the nurses was attaching to the patient. She listened carefully as Len's clothes were cut off and Nathan carried out his primary survey, with each member of the team calling out necessary information. The designated scribe recorded everything on the Trauma Sheet, including relevant timings, plus drugs, fluids and treatments given.

'Airway clear, bilateral air entry…both lungs sound fine. Pupils normal and reactive. No sign of any upper body, neck or spinal injuries.'

Annie acknowledged the information, gathering updates on Len's blood pressure, pulse, sats and respiration rate. Gus, aided by Gail, had gained additional IV access, and was administering the fluids Annie had requested to counteract Len's shock and blood loss. Gus had also drawn up blood for cross-matching and for the tests she asked for, including full blood count, urea and electrolyte concentrations, as well as blood gases. A nurse runner was ready to go to the lab for those tests not able to be done in Resus, to request the cross-matching and order units of blood.

'Gus, can you see to a urinary catheter next?' Annie asked.

The young doctor nodded, accepting the items he needed from the trolley Gail had made ready before the patient's arrival. 'I'm on it now.'

'Thanks.'

'We're going to need that orthopod down here.'

The sound of Nathan's voice caused a ripple of aware-ness to run through her, but Annie fought against her reaction to him. 'What have you got?' she asked, moving closer as he delivered his verdict on the patient's lower limb injuries.

'Open tib and fib fractures of both lower legs, disloca-tion of the right patella, and the right femur is broken…probably in two places. X-rays will confirm the extent of the damage. We also need an idea of any pelvic injury before he can go up to surgery, but first I need to stem the femoral bleed at the site of this deep laceration,' Nathan informed her, concentrating on his task to halt the haemorrhage in the man's right thigh.

Annie couldn't help but admire Nathan's skill and calm composure. He was just as special a doctor as she remem-bered, always unflappable, whatever the extent and urgency of the crisis. She trusted him completely in terms of his clinical judgement, technique and treatment of patients. It was his treatment of her heart that had been so lacking. Thrusting that painful thought aside, she ensured that the replacement fluids were running correctly, then checked the stats and the time elapsed since the patient had been under their care.

'How's the bleed?'

'Under control now. I just need to get this tied off. Thanks, Holly,' Nathan added, as the competent young staff nurse assisted him. 'Len's going to need a lot of work in Theatre.' He glanced up, and her breath caught for a second as she met his gaze. 'I'd recommend a femoral nerve block.'

'Yes, I agree. Then we can get his legs splinted before X-ray.'

Nathan accepted the syringe Holly handed him, checked the dosage, then deftly inserted the needle, injecting lidocaine in a fan pattern in the thigh. 'Any idea how long the radiographer will be, Annie?'

'I'm here,' a voice announced, and Francesca Scott strode into the resus bay, pulling on her protective lead apron.

Tall and athletic, a riot of red corkscrew curls somehow constrained in the thick plait that fell to her waist, Francesca was unfairly dubbed the Ice Maiden by some of the hospital staff. Annie had always got on well with the other woman, however, and admired her friend's skill and kindness to her patients.

Despite her more senior role, Annie remained silent and allowed Nathan to outline the extent of Len's injuries. Once the femoral block had done its job, and splints had been fitted, Francesca went to work using the overhead emergency X-ray equipment now in use in the A and E department. As well as the standard precautionary lateral cervical spine and frontal chest images, she took specific pictures of Len's pelvis and legs.

'Can you scan his abdomen and pelvic region, too?' Annie asked. 'We're querying any internal blood loss.'

Using the portable ultrasound, Francesca complied with the request, and within minutes the X-ray and scan images came up on the diagnostic screen.

'The leg fractures are clear and extensive. But there's no sign of pelvic fracture or internal bleeding, and no free fluids in the abdominal cavity. I think it's just bruising,' Francesca suggested, moving aside so that Annie and Nathan could assess the various images for themselves.

Annie frowned. The X-rays were pretty gruesome. One fibula had jagged splits and fragments in several places, while the other, and both tibias, had multiple but thankfully cleaner breaks. As Nathan had predicted, the right femur had snapped in two places—mid-shaft and just above the knee that had dislocated, its patella misplaced high and to one side, the joint swollen and distorted.

Annie was acutely aware of Nathan close to her. For an unguarded moment she found herself leaning in to inhale his unique and subtle musky aroma, masculine, sensuous and once so familiar. Horrified at her weakness, she straightened and struggled to concentrate on her job. She studiously watched the monitor readings, calling for more blood units as Len was slow to respond to the fluids he'd been given.

Thankfully, the orthopaedic registrar arrived then, tutting over the X-rays. 'We'll operate straight away,' he said, before setting off with copies of the notes and images to brief his department's senior consultant.

'OK,' Annie called, organising her team for their final duties. 'Let's get ready to transfer Len up to surgery. Thanks, Francesca. Good job, everyone.'

A further flurry of activity ensued before Len, stable but serious, was on his way to the theatre team, who would take over his care and do all they could to repair the damage to his legs.

Having taken off her protective clothing, Annie went with Holly to see the family, to explain what had happened and what was going to be done during surgery. She left Holly to escort the anxious relatives upstairs to the waiting area in the surgical suite, while she returned to Resus, noting that the first bay was still occupied. Robert and his team were still battling to save the elderly woman whose heart problems had led to the accident.

Her own team had already dispersed, to deal with less serious casualties in the main department, while a nurse remained to ensure Resus Bay Two was prepared for the next emergency. Annie paused a moment, unsettled by her feelings as she looked at Nathan. He was sitting on a stool, finishing his notes, but he smiled when he saw her, causing an uncomfortable knot to form in her chest.

'It's only my second day here, but already I am very impressed by the whole department.'

'We're a close-knit unit,' she agreed, pleased for her colleagues at Nathan's praise.

She scanned the notes he handed her and signed off on them, clutching the folder to her like a shield as she took a step backwards, aware that they were now alone.

'It was like old times working with you, Annie. You've developed into one hell of a doctor.' The husky edge to his voice sent a tingle down her spine. 'And we haven't lost that natural understanding.'

She had always enjoyed being teamed with Nathan in the past. He was naturally talented, never losing his cool in any situation, and always maintaining his compassion for the patient and his generosity towards the staff working with him. Despite her painful awareness of him, for a while there, engrossed in meeting Len's needs, it was as if the years apart had never happened. Working in tandem, displaying the kind of instinctive understanding that only grew with trust and time, she and Nathan had been attuned to each other's thoughts and actions. And that had been scary. She couldn't allow Nathan to ease back into her life as if nothing had happened. It had hurt too much last time. Bare minutes after seeing him again and she was already vulnerable. She had to do whatever was necessary to protect herself, because no way could she risk her heart taking a second beating.

In consequence, she kept her voice controlled when she

replied. 'All that was a long time ago. I'm surprised you're
not a hotshot consultant by now, Nathan. I thought that was
all you wanted,' she added, unable to keep the bitter edge
from her voice, but regretting her challenge as the friendliness faded from Nathan's expression, his eyes turning
hard and shuttered.

'You had no idea what I wanted, Annie. You never
shared my hopes and dreams and fears because you
weren't interested in anything but what *you* wanted.'

'That's not fair.'

'Really?' One eyebrow lifted sardonically. 'What do
you know about me? What do you know about my life, my
goals, my feelings?'

Alarmed, wishing she had never begun this awful conversation, Annie focused on her own years of hurt. 'So why
did you put up with me then, if I was so selfish?'

'Because I loved you. Apparently that wasn't good
enough. It had to be your way or no way.'

She stared at him, speechless with shock, both at the
pain-laden softness of his words and the fact that he so
clearly believed what he'd said. But he *hadn't* loved her,
an inner voice cried in agonised remembrance. Had he?
Tears stung her eyes. If it *was* true, why had he rejected
her? A wave of indignation swelled within her, only to vie
with a disconcerting flicker of doubt. Enough doubt that
she swallowed the rush of argumentative words that fought
for freedom…words she would once have been unable to
contain. She was older now. She had a responsible position.
She wasn't going to lower herself by reacting childishly.
Squaring her shoulders, she took a steadying breath and
refused to respond further, all too worried that Nathan's accusations would play on her mind in the days ahead.

'We're clearly not going to agree, and rehashing things

serves no purpose,' she stated, proud of the coolness she'd managed to inject into her voice, betraying no sign of the way she was shaking inside. 'I suggest we get back to work. We have other patients to see.'

Eager to put distance between herself and Nathan, she left Resus and returned Len's case folder to its proper place, so the Trauma Sheet could be photocopied for the in-house notes. She was grateful that the department was so busy, hoping she could lose herself in work and ignore her confused thoughts about Nathan's troubling reappearance in her life…not to mention his very different recollection about their time together and their distressing parting.

In truth, she had been on edge since Frazer and Callie's wedding. A doctor and paramedic respectively, on the local air ambulance crew, her friends had married at Strathlochan Castle on Christmas Eve, with Annie as maid of honour. The day had ended with Callie's bridal bouquet flying through the air and landing squarely in Annie's reluctant arms. A shiver ran through her as she relived the moment. At the time she had felt uneasy, as if it was a bad omen instead of the good luck tradition proclaimed. Now, three weeks later, Nathan had shown up, confirming her premonition.

Whilst Annie had been thrilled at her friends' happiness, their wedding had brought back memories, making her wonder what her own life would have been like had things turned out differently. The reality was that she was now unlikely ever to marry and have the family she had always longed for. Nathan had stolen her dreams when he'd broken her heart, and she would never trust another man again.

Maybe things had happened for the best. She'd certainly progressed much further in her career than she had expected, because she had used hard work as an escape, a

comfort, a protection against the pain. The kind of debili-
tating pain she never wanted to experience again. Even now
it hurt too much to think of what could have been—what
should have been, had Nathan loved her as much as she had
loved him. As much as he now claimed to have done. She
had to remember old hurts and be wise to the lessons of
the past, lest she fall for Nathan's charm all over again.

Conscious of him watching her, she made her way to
Reception, collected information on the next patient
waiting to be seen and called her through from the crowded
waiting area. Focusing on the young child—who had
somehow managed to wedge a couple of polystyrene
packing chips up her nose, where they were well and truly
stuck—Annie determined to set the problem of Nathan
from her mind. At least for the time being. Unfortunately,
though, however much she might wish it, she didn't think
he was going to go away any time soon.

Consumed with frustration, Nathan watched Annie draw
a curtain around the cubicle into which she had shown a
worried mother with a tearful young daughter.

Every time he was close to Annie his heart started ham-
mering in his chest, his breath felt trapped in his lungs, and
his palms dampened. Let alone what happened further
south, his body tightening and hardening in an instinctive
reaction to her presence. She still aroused in him equal
parts physical, gut-tingling desire and crippling emotional
uncertainty, just as in the past.

Five years on they still had a connection, and worked
well together on a professional basis, but it was clear he
was going to have a difficult time making any headway
with Annie personally. It had been a mistake to be drawn
into a disagreement so soon. He shouldn't have let her rile

him. But her stubbornness and her inability to see another point of view drove him to distraction.

Sucking in a breath, he struggled for calm. There was so much he and Annie needed to talk about, to resolve. That they were far apart in their perception of the events of the past was obvious, and it was not going to be easy to get her to listen. However, he had to try. If he ever hoped to move on, with or without her, he needed to settle things in his head…and his heart…once and for all. But none of that was going to happen immediately. Until he could get Annie alone, away from the hospital, he needed to focus on the job and devote his full attention to the patients who needed him.

The next few hours sped by, as he worked through the assorted cases assigned to him. A series of common and familiar complaints, such as infections, angina, sprains, fractures, cuts and an asthma attack, were interspersed with two further calls on him to join the resus team. The first was a serious road accident, involving several cars on the motorway, which brought the A and E department almost to breaking point. The second serious incident involved a twenty-year-old man who had suffered a worrying head injury in a fall from some scaffolding. As soon as he was stable enough, he had been transferred by air ambulance to the neurological unit in Glasgow.

Nathan was well aware that Annie was avoiding him. He doubted she would have voluntarily worked with him at all had it not been for the resus emergencies and Robert Mowbray's directive that she help him settle in. He didn't need a minder, but anything that placed him around Annie was good. Her reaction to the consultant's decision and her sharp words after they had treated Len Gordon had been the only hints of weakness, the only signs that his presence here disturbed her in any way and she was not as indifferent as she would have him believe.

It was early afternoon by the time he had a chance for a break to grab a quick lunch. His stomach rumbled. Breakfast seemed a lifetime ago, and then he'd only managed a banana and a glass of fruit smoothie because he'd been so churned up about seeing Annie again. Annie was nowhere in sight in the department, or in the staffroom, so he decided to try the canteen in the hope of catching up with her there. Seeing Olivia Barr waiting by the lifts, Nathan pushed open a door marked 'staff only' and slipped into the seldom-used rear stairway, determined to avoid the predatory nurse and her unwelcome attentions.

Aside from the fact that Olivia hadn't let an opportunity go by in the last two days to come on to him, he had doubts about her as a nurse. During his short time in the department he had seen that although she had good clinical skills—when she focused on her tasks—she wasn't a team player. And the way she spoke to and interacted with some patients left a great deal to be desired. On a personal level he had rejected several advances, making it clear that he was not interested and that if she persisted he would have no choice but to be blunt. Olivia represented everything he found unattractive in a woman, from her vampish flirting and sly insincerity to her falsely pouting lips, heavy make-up and silicone-enhanced breasts. Annie, by contrast, was the embodiment of everything that was natural and feminine, with no artificiality about her.

Annie…

As if he had conjured her up from his thoughts, he had just reached the landing of the floor that housed the canteen when the door opened, forcing him to step back, and Annie emerged into the otherwise deserted stairway. He noted her startled expression when she saw him, her nervousness apparent as the door closed behind her and she realised they were alone. She glanced around, clearly searching for some avenue of escape, but he wasn't about to allow it. Who knew when he'd have another chance to catch her attention?

As she backed up against the door, he slowly closed the distance between them. 'You've been avoiding me, Annie.'

Her chin lifted in defiance at his challenge, but she wouldn't meet his gaze. 'I've been doing my job—not thinking about you at all.'

'Right.' Stepping closer, he flattened both his hands on the door, one either side of her head. 'So there's nothing to stop you spending some time with me now?'

'I have to get back to the department. You know how crazy it is today,' she excused, the unsteady note in her voice betraying her unease.

'Meet with me later, then.'

'I can't.' He saw the irregular beat of her pulse at the hollow of her throat, noted the bloom of colour warm her ivory skin. 'There's no point in this, Nathan.'

He couldn't resist leaning closer, so he could savour her tantalising jasmine scent. 'There's every point,' he argued, everything in him craving a taste of her, something he had been denied and had yearned for for five long years.

'Nathan…'

'We need to talk, Annie,' he insisted, not prepared to be fobbed off this time.

Her own palms flattened on his chest and he revelled in the contact, even though it was meant to hold him at bay. 'No!'

'Yes.' He refused to allow her to ignore reality. 'We have to face the past…if only to move on.'

'I've already moved on, Nathan,' she insisted, but to him her words lacked conviction.

'Have you? Really?' She might *think* she believed that, but he didn't—no matter what she said to the contrary. 'All we had together must have meant little to you if you could throw it away with such cavalier disregard.' And care so little for its loss, he added silently. He leaned in closer, seeing anxiety darken her blue eyes, feeling the increasing pressure of her hands on his chest as she tried to keep distance between them. 'I haven't moved on, Annie. I don't think you have any idea what you leaving like that did to me, or what kind of hell I've been in for five years. Maybe you tell yourself you don't even care. You've invented your own version of reality to help justify to yourself the fact that you tossed us aside. But your perception of events is very different from mine. Well, reality bites, sweetheart, and the time has come for us to settle this.'

As if Nathan's words were not enough to panic her, Annie froze as he moved one hand. His palm cupped her cheek, the caress of his fingers sending a trail of heat across her skin and firing every nerve-ending to zinging awareness. His thumb under her chin tilted her face up until she could no longer avoid his gaze. Robbed of speech by the intense expression in his dark eyes, she couldn't form a single protest. Nor could she look away. He stared down at her, brooding and mysterious, his closeness making her pulse race and preventing her dragging enough air into parched lungs.

'How is it possible that you are even more beautiful than ever?'

His husky words sent waves of arousal washing through her, tightening her insides and speeding her pulse. Terrified of her reaction to him, she fruitlessly endeavoured to hold him off, to create some more space to breathe, to think. Every part of her was on red alert—his touch, his nearness, his musky male scent all combining to rob her of common sense and strip away her resistance.

'Nathan…'

Her warning stalled, his name escaping on a whisper of breath rather than sounding like the denial she had intended. And when the pad of his thumb grazed across the swell of her lower lip she couldn't maintain coherent thought. As he closed the remaining centimetres between them, his fingers sliding back to fist in her hair and hold her still, she forgot every reason why they shouldn't do this. Instead, her traitorous lips were already parted in eager anticipation when his own brushed across them. She responded instinctively as his mouth captured hers, demanding, needy, plunging her back into the once familiar abyss of heady excitement and unquenchable desire.

Annie had forgotten how incredible Nathan's seductive, erotic kisses were. No, that was wrong. She hadn't forgotten…she had blanked the memories out, because they caused her so much pain and hopeless longing. But her body remembered his taste, the perfection of his touch, the earth-shattering pleasure only he brought her. For an endless moment she ignored everything but the here and now. Unable to help herself, she moved in closer still, craving tighter contact, feeling the delicious jolt as her breasts pressed against the wall of his chest, stimulating the hardened peaks of her nipples. A moan escaped as Nathan's free hand cupped her rear and drew her against him. His hips rocked into her, making her all too conscious of the hard length of his arousal, and an answering hollow knot tightened deep inside her in response. She rubbed herself over him, desperate to assuage the empty ache of need.

The hungry kiss deepened, turning almost feral in its urgent intensity. Their raging passion was immediately rekindled, flaring hotter than ever. Annie met and matched Nathan's every move, every stroke, every suck… her teeth nipping, her tongue duelling, twining and teasing with his. She wallowed in the sense of being reborn, of coming home, her body primed, begging for the fulfilment only he could give her.

Then, somewhere below them, the sound of a door closing reverberated in the stillness. Footsteps echoed on the concrete stairs, snapping Annie back to the reality of where she was, what she was doing and *who* she was doing it with. With a cry of distress she wrenched away, fighting against Nathan's hold.

'Stop!' she gasped.

She couldn't do this. Couldn't allow Nathan's potent sex appeal to sweep away all the pain, anger and despair of the last five years as if nothing had happened. It was over. It *was*! As Nathan reluctantly released her she stepped away, her legs feeling too weak and rubbery to hold her up. She'd chosen to take the back stairs in an attempt to avoid him, yet had only succeeded in trapping herself alone with him in a secluded spot for long enough to forget every powerful reason she must keep him at a distance.

'There's unfinished business between us, Annie. Somehow, somewhere, we are going to deal with it,' he warned her.

His intent was clear, and it scared her, because she couldn't handle seeing him or raking up the past, knowing she was still vulnerable to him.

'You didn't want—'

'You have no idea what I wanted…you never did,' he interrupted heatedly, dragging a hand through his wayward hair. 'And you certainly didn't stay around long enough that last day to listen to my point of view. Then you refused to see or speak to me. I loved you, but you ripped out my heart and stomped all over it, turning your back on everything we were to each other, tossing it away as if it was nothing.'

Tears filled her eyes and she held up a hand, backing away. 'You're wrong!'

'No, I'm not.' His tone was uncompromising and he refused to allow her retreat, despite the footsteps coming closer up the stairs. 'I deserve my say—you owe me that much at least.'

'I have to go,' she insisted, shaking her head, denying his words, anxiety tying her nerves into knots.

'I'm not letting you run this time, Annie.'

But that was just what she did. Ran from him. Shaking, scared and confused, she pushed past him and rushed down the stairs as fast as her wobbly legs could carry her, deaf to the greeting of the admin assistant she passed on the flight below. The woman's presence had brought a much-needed return of sanity, preventing her from something even more reckless than the explosive kiss. She had to get away from Nathan—had to have some time alone to regroup and restore her shattered equilibrium.

With one touch, one kiss, the barriers she had thought impenetrable had been rent asunder. Despite everything that had happened, all the pain he had caused her, Nathan still brought her to her knees and sent her hormones crazy with insatiable desire. She had to do something to prevent herself from falling for him and being hurt all over again.

Slipping unnoticed through a side fire exit, Annie hurried outside the hospital building, moving around the corner out of sight of anyone coming and going from the car park, the A and E department, or the separate building nearby that housed the maternity unit.

Oblivious to the cold, she leaned against the wall, her

whole body trembling. As she drew in several deep breaths in an effort to compose herself the fingers of one hand strayed to her mouth. Her lips, puffy and sensitised from the wildness of the kiss, still tingled in reaction, and she could still savour Nathan's taste on her tongue. Closing her eyes, she groaned, reliving the last few minutes in Technicolor detail.

Dear heaven, what had she done?

And what on earth was she going to do now?

All she could think about was the urgent need to protect herself against Nathan's potent effect on her. He had stormed back into her life and clearly planned to turn it upside down, demanding that they confront their painful past. Why now? What did he hope to achieve? And why couldn't she put his accusations that *she* had broken *his* heart out of her mind? There had been no denying the hurt in his eyes. And his suggestion that she had never given him the chance to explain his point of view nagged at her. She squared her shoulders, struggling to maintain her own sense of being wronged. What was there to explain? Nathan hadn't wanted her. He'd made that obvious when he'd rejected her. How could he now try to turn it around and imply *she* was at fault?

But he had—and he was here for reasons of his own, refusing to let it go.

Somehow she had to erect a façade that even Nathan couldn't penetrate. It was the only way she could survive. There certainly couldn't be a repeat of what had just happened on the stairs. Her instant surrender to his kiss had proved just how vulnerable she was to him.

But what could she do?

A sudden plan came to mind.

Desperate, she pulled her mobile phone out of her

pocket, turned it on and sent an SOS message to the one person she could trust to save her from herself and stop her from making a monumental mistake.

CHAPTER THREE

'Is the damage very bad, Doctor?'

Nathan looked up from his examination of the burns on the elderly woman's hand, hoping to ease the pain and anxiety reflected in her cloudy blue eyes. 'You did the right thing getting your hand under cold water straight away, Mrs Mooney, and wrapping it in clingfilm before coming to the hospital gave further protection against infection. Not doing so could have made the resulting injuries worse.'

'Lucky I took note of all those television programmes,' she offered with a brave smile.

'You did well. Aside from the blisters, there are a couple of partial thickness burns, but nothing that appears to be deeper,' he reassured her, gently turning the injured hand over again and reassessing the situation, carefully checking between the fingers. 'We'll give you some pain relief, then we'll clean things up and remove any dead skin, drain the blisters, and put on some cream before dressing the hand. Do you have someone at home with you?' he asked, concerned that the woman wouldn't manage alone.

'Yes, I live with my daughter and her children.'

'Then you'll be able to go home when we're done.' He gave her non-injured hand a squeeze. 'But you'll need to come back to the outpatient clinic tomorrow, to have the dressing changed and the hand reassessed. After that your GP surgery will be able to manage your aftercare. Is your tetanus cover up to date?'

Mrs Mooney's lined face creased further as she frowned. 'Goodness, I can't remember when I last had a vaccination.'

'Don't worry. We'll give you another injection to be sure. Could you take care of that please, Holly?' he requested, glancing up at the quietly efficient young staff nurse.

'Of course, Dr Shepherd. No problem.'

The pretty blonde manoeuvred a trolley next to him, on which she had laid out all the items he required to treat and dress Mrs Mooney's hand. 'Thanks.'

'Your grandchildren are quite a handful, are they, Mrs Mooney?'

Nathan heard Holly's question, grateful to her for keeping the worried patient's mind occupied as he checked that the pain relief had done its job so he could begin to clean and dress her wounds. Concentrating on his task, he listened with half an ear as Mrs Mooney responded to Holly's calm friendliness.

'Yes, indeed, Nurse.' She gave a raspy chuckle. 'You need eyes in the back of your head with those boys. That's how this happened. I only turned away for a moment to pick up the youngest, who had fallen on the floor. When I looked round his brother had climbed onto a kitchen chair and was pulling the kettle towards him.'

Mrs Mooney's hand trembled at the memory, and Nathan paused until she settled again before inserting the needle to aspirate the first of the blisters, drawing fluid into the syringe.

'Anyway,' she continued, 'I set the baby down, rushed

to the counter and managed to pull Johnny aside before he hurt himself. Unfortunately my other arm caught the kettle, spilling the boiling water on my hand.'

'Ouch.' Holly tutted in sympathy.

'I'm just glad the children weren't burned. I didn't even think what I was doing. I just acted on instinct and couldn't help myself. Do you know what I mean, Doctor?'

As he finished cleaning, aspirating and debriding the damaged areas of the hand, Nathan nodded. 'I do, Mrs Mooney.'

Hadn't he done the very same thing himself a few hours ago? Despite knowing the timing was wrong, he'd kissed Annie with all the desperation and urgency clamouring within him. He'd been unable to stop, even though he'd known it was too soon to push her to face what remained between them. It had been foolish, but inevitable. And he'd been burned in a very different kind of way, succeeding only in spooking Annie, causing her to strengthen the barriers she had erected against him.

But the need and longing to touch her and taste her had tormented him for five years. When presented with the opportunity, after being deprived of her for so long, the temptation had been too great for him to resist. Now he had set his cause back even further, making the goal he had come here to achieve harder than ever.

Smothering a sigh, he glanced up at the clock on the cubicle wall. His shift had officially ended half an hour ago, but he'd never been one to clock off to time. His presence was determined by his patients' needs. A few doctors and nurses might walk off and hand their patient over to another member of staff coming on duty, but that had never been his way. The nature of accident and emergency medicine involved a rapid turnaround of multiple patients, but within that he believed in giving the best continuity of care possible, and he tried to see each case through to the end.

Annie had held the same philosophy. He could only hope that hadn't changed, and that he would still have a chance to catch up with her before she left for home. Seeing her was a necessity—as was pinning her down so they could talk away from the lack of privacy and the pressures of the hospital.

Returning his attention to Mrs Mooney, grateful that she appeared less distressed, and knowing that was as much due to Holly's expert care as anything else, Nathan applied some silver sulphadiazine cream to the injured hand before using sterile non-adherent dressings and covering the whole hand with a special glove which was secured around the wrist. That done, he stripped off his surgical gloves and tossed them in the bin.

After prescribing some analgesia and anti-inflammatory medication for her to take at home for any pain, and a precautionary antibiotic to stem any infection, he left Holly tidying the cubicle and escorted Mrs Mooney out. Her worried daughter waited with the two boisterous boys. Nathan gave them some reassurance, and a few last-minute instructions for her care, then returned to finish up the notes and have a word with Holly before leaving.

'You've been great, Holly…thanks for all your help today.'

Surprise and gratitude were evident in the young woman's expression. 'Thank you, Nathan.'

Her shy smile failed to lift the lingering sadness that shadowed her eyes, and he paused a moment, unsure whether to say anything more. Several times during the day he had sensed tension between Holly and junior doctor Gus Buchanan, and he had wondered what the story was. He hated to see anyone unhappy, but at the same time didn't feel he had been in the department long enough to intrude—not without knowing more about the dynamics, anyway. Shaking his head, he said goodnight and made his way towards the staffroom. He'd keep an eye on Holly just in case. Being there for other people was the story of his life—something he had long resented when it had been forced upon him, but a trait he was unwilling to break when it came to patients, colleagues and friends. Right now, however, he had enough problems of his own to sort out, and for once he had to put himself first.

There were several people in the staffroom. Thankfully, the predatory Olivia Barr was not one of them, but then neither was Annie. He'd checked when returning the notes on his final patient and knew she was only minutes ahead of him. A few discreet queries and he discovered she was in the women's locker room, changing. Feeling nervous and uncomfortable, he loitered in the corridor, pretending to read the messages pinned higgledy-piggledy on the staff noticeboard. Knowing he couldn't give Annie too much time to think and harden her heart even further against him, he was determined to catch her before she left the hospital.

As he waited, he thought back to the moment he had first seen Annie. He would never forget it.

By the time he had negotiated a temporary escape from the ties of home and managed to get to medical school he had found himself a few years older than the other students in his intake. Having always felt alone, never having connected with or been part of a group, he had approached those early days at medical school with a mix of intense apprehension and an unbelievable sense of freedom. At last he had been doing what *he* wanted with his life, and he had been able to put himself first—at least for part of the time.

In medical school he'd had no one else depending on him, making demands on him, holding him back.

From day one he had been drawn to Annie Webster. Young and full of life, something about her had reached out to the lonely man inside him, the hidden part of him no one knew but which craved someone to love…yearned even more for someone to love him. One look at Annie's captivating face, laughing blue eyes and widely smiling mouth and he'd lost his heart. During the first months of training she had still been involved with a boyfriend from home, so Nathan had smothered any hopes of more between them. But they had formed a deep friendship. The first of his life. Her enthusiasm and determination to be a doctor had matched his own, but she'd struggled with some of the study demands. He'd been pleased to help, receiving so much more back by basking in Annie's sunshine, her joyousness and zest for life.

Then she'd been free, her relationship having failed to survive the distance, and having grown apart from her school sweetheart as their lives went in different directions. She had been sad, but not heartbroken, and after a decent interval Nathan had plucked up the nerve to ask her out. To his amazement she'd said yes. Head-over-heels, they had soon moved in together. Annie had made his world whole for the first time ever—only to destroy it four years later, when he had refused to immediately agree to her unreasonable demand. His own plea to discuss it further had fallen on deaf ears. She had left him—and the hospital—with no warning and without a backward glance.

He had made a mistake by not confiding more in Annie about his past and his home life. He could acknowledge that now. But she had never asked anything about him. She had accepted him for who he was and, addicted to her, enjoying the novelty and freedom to be himself, he'd never volunteered the information. It had been as if there were two Nathans—the one weighed down with the responsibility and shackles of home, forced to grow up years before his time, and Annie's Nathan, happy, loved, following his dreams. He hadn't wanted sad, dour, friendless Nathan to spoil what he had with Annie, and so he had followed her example to live each day as it came, embracing life and enjoying the moment.

And so they had gone on, as emotionally and physically close as two people could be. Yet while Annie had been open, exposing every part of herself and drawing him into her life and her family, he had revealed little about the man beneath the surface. That was his fault. Had she known of his background it might have made a difference that last day. It might have made her understand his instinctive reaction to her demand. But she had never asked or given any sign she wanted to know anything more about him as a person. And he had been insecure, scared—a part of him always waiting for her to tell him he wasn't good enough for her, in his own heart believing he didn't deserve her.

Now, five years on, he had been released from the burdens of his past and could face life as *he* wanted to, with no one else to think about or provide for. It was time to reach for his own goals and needs. And so he had come to find Annie, to discover if they could reclaim what they had lost or, if it was truly over, to lay it to rest so he could move on once and for all. Today had made it clear that his feelings had not diminished and he loved Annie as much as ever. She was as essential to his life as breathing. It was equally clear that Annie had woven her own view of the past—one that would be hard to challenge because, however distorted from reality, she believed it. He had to try to open her mind and her heart.

And so he was here, waiting, hurting, needing…hoping against hope for a second chance with the only woman he had ever loved. The woman who held his fate and the shattered fragments of his heart in her hands.

'Damn.'

Annie cursed under her breath as she cracked open the door of the locker room and peeped out. Spying Nathan waiting near the noticeboard, blocking her route towards the exit, she carefully closed the door and leaned back on it, barely resisting the urge to bang her head against the adjacent wall. She should have known she couldn't evade him so easily.

How long was he going to wait her out? He was dogged in his determination once he set his mind to something. Restless, she paced across the small, thankfully deserted room, a frown on her face as she checked her bag. Fastening her locker and pocketing the key, she placed her discarded scrubs in the container provided, as always approving of the hospital board's policies regarding infection control and cleanliness. Thankfully Strathlochan had an excellent record in tackling and preventing superbugs, but no one could afford to be too careful or become complacent.

Impatient, Annie glanced at her watch. It was past time to leave. There had been no response to her earlier SOS text message and she was worried. What if it hadn't got through? What if her plan failed before it even started? She really didn't want another face-to-face with Nathan alone.

Setting her bag at her feet, she sat down on a wooden bench near the door, hoping no one else would come in…hoping that Nathan would just *go*. The same questions that had plagued her all day still pounded in her head. Why was he here? Why now, after five years, did he want to rake over the past? Why had he kissed her? Worse, why had she kissed him back with such mindless passion?

No answers eased her troubled mind and she sighed, one hand rubbing the back of her neck, where tension had tightened her muscles. The strain of the day was catching up with her. She was tired, and wanted nothing more than to go home and have a long soak in a hot, fragrant bubble bath before falling into bed. The oblivion of sleep had never seemed more attractive. After the incident on the stairs she had been a nervous wreck throughout the rest of her busy shift. Half the time had been spent worrying whether her risky emergency plan would work and the other half trying to avoid Nathan as much as possible. It hadn't helped that the feel and taste and scent of him had lingered to torment and tempt her.

She huffed out a breath, her errant thoughts turning to her first days of medical school and meeting Nathan. She had been eighteen, bursting with enthusiasm and an almost naïve zeal. Most of the rest of the students in the group had been around the same age...all except Nathan. At twenty-two he had stood apart, serious, already seeming much more mature and interesting than the rest of the intake.

On the surface he had been reserved and shy, a very private person. He had kept to himself, but as they had become friends and he'd relaxed more around her she had discovered that he was caring, intelligent, warm and surprisingly funny. He had also been generous with his time and knowledge, always willing to help her when she struggled with areas of the coursework. She was at her best with people, while Nathan, although having a special touch with patients, was gifted academically, preferring to focus on his studies and avoid the social merry-go-round, where he had seemed awkward and out of place. They had made a good team, and the relationship had blossomed into so much more when she had accepted Nathan's tentative invitation to date. Friendship had led to passion…and to four years of happiness together.

She would never forget the first time they had made love. She'd had only one serious boyfriend before Nathan, and, whilst she had enjoyed sex, she'd soon realised how innocent and tame her previous experience had been. For Joe *had* been a boy, and nothing had prepared her for Nathan the man—for all he'd done to her and made her feel…out of control and soaring to the heavens with indescribable pleasure. Nathan had indulged and encouraged her adventurous spirit, and she had met and matched his fiery passion, the challenge to explore and experiment and push the boundaries. Nathan's sensual wickedness had been a delicious surprise. She'd teased him about it always being the quiet ones who had hidden depths. He'd just smiled that slow, sexy smile, and then shown her over and over again how very sinful he could be.

Annie frowned as she considered how it had all gone so wrong. Nathan's rejection of her stung as painfully now as it had then. She hadn't understood him at all, she realised. And there was so much about him that she still didn't know. Her frown deepened. She had been so happy. Nothing else had seemed important. And Nathan had never volunteered information about his background. It hadn't mattered. Or so she had thought. They'd been in love, the perfect couple, and she had believed they would be together for ever. Until it had all come crashing down around her, leaving her broken and bewildered, her dreams and her heart in tatters.

Now, a few short hours after Nathan's shocking reappearance in her life, her body was rousing itself from a long-enforced slumber and letting her know how enjoyable it would be to renew their acquaintance. She suppressed the shiver of desire that rippled through her and shook her head. That was so *not* going to happen. She had barely survived the last time. If she allowed Nathan to get close again it would destroy her. Despite everything she had made something of herself—something different than she had once planned, but more than she had ever expected. She couldn't let Nathan take that from her.

Hearing a faint rumble of voices from beyond the door, Annie cracked it open again to peep out, and saw two figures further down the corridor. Relief swelled inside her when she saw who Nathan was talking to. Thank God. Please let this plan work, she begged silently, rising to her feet, shouldering her bag and draping her coat over one arm. Hoping that nothing would go wrong in the next few moments, she left the room. It was show time. Disaster management was the name of the game—to give her some breathing space until she came up with a viable long-term solution.

A sound drew Nathan's attention and he turned round, disappointed to discover that it was not Annie emerging from the locker room. Instead, a man he didn't recognise was now loitering further down the corridor. In his late twenties, Nathan judged, the man had short, spiky blond hair, and was dressed in a well-worn black leather jacket, faded jeans with rips across one thigh, and studded black boots. Unable to detect any hospital ID, and cautious about security after his spells in big city hospitals, Nathan moved towards the man, unconsciously putting himself between Annie in the locker room and any hint of a possible problem.

'Can I help you?' he asked, keeping his tone unchallenging.

The man turned to face him with an infectious smile. 'No. Thanks, though. I'm waiting for someone. I—' He broke off, his gaze straying beyond Nathan. 'Ah, here she is!' His smile widened to a grin as a door banged shut and footsteps sounded on the floor.

Nathan just had time to look behind him and move aside as Annie, dressed now in figure-hugging jeans and a blue fleecy top, whooshed past him and straight into the man's arms.

Annie flung herself at Will, hearing his grunt of surprise. Thankfully he caught her, his strong arms closing around her just as she needed them to right now.

'Not that I'm sorry to see you, hon, but what the hell is all this about?' he whispered in her ear as he spun her round.

'Please, *please* play along,' she murmured back, hugging him tight, some of her initial relief giving way to a strange confusion and a sense of unease. 'I'll explain later.'

Slowly Will set her feet back on the floor, keeping an arm around her as she snuggled close. She was horribly aware of Nathan nearby, watching them, and whilst this had been her plan since sending the SOS text, she felt edgy and awkward as she sucked in a steadying breath and introduced the two men.

'Um, Will—this is Nathan Shepherd. He's just joined the unit. Nathan, this is Will Brown, another of the A and E doctors,' she managed, unable to meet Nathan's gaze.

Will reached round her to shake Nathan's hand. 'The name rings a bell.' He smiled, and Annie froze, hoping he wasn't going to do anything embarrassing or say something to give her away.

'Not the foot fetish guy?' he mused. 'Wait a minute. Doughnuts!'

Annie smothered a groan.

Nathan knew his expression was brittle, but he couldn't help it—couldn't have forced a smile if his life had depended on it. Everything inside him seemed to have gone into cold storage. He hadn't thought it was possible to hurt more than he had, but he had been wrong. Fresh pain cut through him, lacerating everything that had dared to begin to live again when he had seen Annie today.

Because Annie was involved with another man.

Clearly she had mentioned him to Will at some time, but was that all that had been noteworthy about their four-year relationship? The doughnuts? It made him feel as if he was just one in a line of unmemorable former boyfriends. Clearly their time together had meant nothing, and she hadn't been as devastated about their break-up or as in love with him as he had thought.

And she'd been out with a foot fetishist?

'Not that your feet aren't cute, hon,' Will was saying now, 'but...'

'Yeah, I know all about your own fetishes!' Annie grinned.

'You sure do!'

Nathan felt sick. He had made one more in a series of dumb mistakes over this woman, and he had no one to blame but himself. Of all the scenarios and outcomes he had considered when he had decided to come here, Annie being with someone else had not been on his list. A stupid oversight—one he had probably subconsciously avoided because of how he felt right at this minute. Lost. Without hope. Gripped by pain. He had been unable to date any other woman, and deep inside he had wanted to believe that

Annie had loved him enough not to give herself to another man. Idiot, idiot, *idiot*, he chastised himself.

And Will was another doctor with whom he would have to work in this department? Just great. He'd have to see them together every day. Why in God's name had he come here? What the hell had he expected to achieve? Had he really thought that Annie would still be thinking of him, pining for him? She'd made her views plain five years ago. Just because he'd never stopped loving her, it didn't mean she felt the same. He could see that—now.

All this time he had clung to the fantasy that he and Annie were destined to be together—that she was his one soul mate and that somehow he could win her back. He was angry that he had been such a pathetic fool. Annie had left him, had said it was over. He had not wanted to believe it. He had taken a chance for the first time in his life of opening himself to another person and Annie had rejected him—had run away at the first hurdle, demanding her own way at once rather than stopping to listen to his point of view or caring about his feelings.

He frowned again as the thoughts raced through his mind, admitting to himself that while there were big parts of him that only Annie had ever seen, there were significant parts of him that he had withheld even from her. She hadn't understood his motivation because he had never explained...but when trouble had come she had run rather than give him the benefit of the doubt, throwing his love back at him as if it meant nothing to her.

He knew that feeling. All his life he had felt rejected, not good enough. Annie had been different, had seen him differently—or so he had thought.

Annie hadn't said one word about Will. Why hadn't she told him right away that she was seeing someone? Even when she had panicked after their passionate kiss earlier in the day, being involved with another man had not featured amongst her excuses before she had run. And none of the staff gossip referred to Annie being attached. Why? What was he missing? Or was he just trying to ignore the fact that Annie's heart now belonged to someone else? He might not have been able to turn to another woman for solace, but that didn't mean Annie had been celibate. Pain stabbed at what remained of his heart. He was just deluding himself, rubbing salt into festering wounds.

It seemed he was still as much of a fool over Annie as he always had been. He'd been carrying her photo and her memory around with him for five long, painfully lonely years. And while he had been acting like a lovesick teenager Annie had moved on with her life…just as she had said. She had never given him a second thought. It hurt. Badly.

'Ready to go home, hon?'

Will's question drew him from his agonising thoughts. Nathan saw Annie glance quickly at him from beneath her lashes, but she refused to meet his gaze.

'Yep. I'm done here,' she replied, turning back towards Will as the man helped her on with her coat.

Wishing he was any place else, Nathan felt as if his feet were rooted to the spot, pain slicing through him as Will, one arm wrapped around Annie's waist, offered a friendly smile he was powerless to return.

'Good to meet you, Nathan. You'll have to come round to our place for a meal one night while you're here.'

He noted the way Annie dug her elbow into Will's ribs. Clearly she didn't appreciate the idea any more than Nathan did. No way could he endure a social evening and make polite conversation with Annie and her lover. As they turned and walked away, Nathan felt a crushing fist destroy the remaining fragments of his heart and he sank back against the wall, needing additional support to keep him standing. He had no business messing with Annie's life. He might want to punch Will's lights out, but it was clear the guy cared about her and who could blame him? She was beautiful, special—and she didn't want him. When was he going to accept the inevitable and give up? Why did he keep punishing himself?

Heading to the men's locker room, glad to find no one else there to witness his misery, he sat down and scrubbed his hands over his face. He had decisions to make. He had half a mind to leave Strathlochan now—tonight. To go and never come back. But he'd signed a contract and, despite his own despair, it wasn't in his nature to let other people down. Besides, where would he go? A bitter, self-mocking laugh escaped him. He didn't belong anywhere now.

Thoughts of Annie had held him together through many nightmares over the years, but she was no longer the solution to his emptiness, no longer the sunshine in his grey world. As much as it killed him to admit it, he could no longer look to her for any kind of future. He was on his own. Alone. As he always had been and as he always would be from now on.

For the moment he would do his job to the best of his abilities and endeavour to keep out of Annie's way… As much as humanly possible, given Robert Mowbray's determination to have them working the same shifts. In the meantime, he would turn down the consultant's suggestion that he lengthen his stay and take a full time position in Strathlochan. Maybe the time had come to consider taking the job he had been offered in Africa…as far away from Annie Webster as he could get.

CHAPTER FOUR

ANNIE was still shaking with reaction by the time they arrived back at the house. Situated midway along a tree-lined terrace, in a quiet part of town not too far from the hospital, the traditional two-storey granite building had been her home since she had arrived in Strathlochan. Aware of Will following her up the path, carrying the fish and chip suppers they had stopped to collect, she fumbled for her keys. The icy evening air stung, and wind-driven raindrops bit into her face like dozens of tiny daggers, reinforcing the fact that winter still held them in its grip. Fingers unsteady, she managed to open the front door, sighing with relief when she stepped inside the welcoming warmth. The house felt more than ever like a sanctuary.

Flipping on the lights, she hung up her coat, dropped her bag at the foot of the stairs, and followed Will through to the homely kitchen. She was grateful for his silence, but knew it would not be long before he asked inevitable questions. Questions she had no wish to answer. In the meantime, she busied herself putting out some fresh salad and filling two glasses with water, while Will served the aromatic fish and chips onto plates. After adding cutlery—and the ketchup Will couldn't seem to consume any food without—they sat at the small table in the kitchen to have their meal.

She rarely matched Will's enjoyment of junk food, but fish and chips were an occasional treat she succumbed to. Tonight, however, Annie had to force herself to eat, her appetite having deserted her. Racked with nerves, she relied on false jollity to cover her muddled emotions, trying to fill the silence as she talked of her day at work, all the time feeling Will watching her.

'Olivia was in full tart mode,' she finished with a forced laugh, as the reality of Nathan's presence as the new doctor in the department would no longer be denied. 'You know what she's like when she senses potential new prey in the vicinity.'

'Annie—'

Pressing on in desperation, she laughed again, knowing she was the one who had touched on dangerous ground and could not now retreat. 'You are so bad! What on earth was that foot fetish stuff about? Did you see Nathan's face? He was so shocked.'

'He was hurt, Annie. More than hurt. I saw that much.' Will reached out and caught her hand as she fiddled with items on the table, unable to sit still or hide her agitation. 'What's going on, hon?'

'Nothing,' she lied, unable to look at him.

His fingers tightened on hers, preventing her efforts to evade him. 'I think you owe me an explanation. I came running in answer to your text, and I went along with the subterfuge you sprang on me.'

'I know, Will. And I'm grateful.' She sighed, the whirl of energy draining away, leaving her weary and unsettled. 'Seeing Nathan today was a big shock and I panicked. All of a sudden he's determined to dig up the past. I don't want to. It's been five years, for goodness' sake!' Apprehension shivered through her as she thought of seeing Nathan in the days ahead. She looked up, facing Will as she voiced her request. 'Help me. Pretend that we're together.'

'I don't think that's a good idea,' Will protested, a frown stripping the customary good humour from his handsome face.

Anxious, she returned the pressure of his fingers. 'Please, Will. For a few days. I need to buy some time while I decide what to do.'

Annie held her breath as she waited for Will to speak, seeing the doubt cloud his eyes as he thought over what she had said. She knew he would do almost anything for her…as she would for him. They had started in Strathlochan's A and E department on the same day, nervous, newly qualified, and embarking on their first foundation year in their chosen specialty of emergency medicine. Both had been singled out and bullied by the then dictatorial and prejudiced senior consultant—thankfully now retired—so it had been natural for them to gravitate together. They had formed an instant bond, swiftly becoming best friends and allies. When, a few months later, Will had split up with his partner and had nowhere to live, Annie had insisted he house-share with her. They'd been living together ever since.

It had worked out perfectly for both of them, with each feeling the other was the sibling they'd never had. They squabbled as much as brother and sister, too, and had different tastes in almost everything. Apart from work, the only interest she and Will shared were the monthly ten-pin bowling matches they enjoyed with friends from the hospital and from other local medical, fire and rescue services. Indeed, the first fixture of the new year was only a couple of days away.

Will, a keen runner, didn't share her passion for cycling and swimming...but Nathan did. Annie loved dogs...so did Nathan. Will was a cat person. He also loved junk food, while Annie tried to eat healthily...the same as Nathan. Why was she even thinking like this? No matter what common ground she and Nathan had shared over books, music, food, the environment and various hobbies, it hadn't made a jot of difference in keeping them together. It hadn't made Nathan love her enough to commit to her. Or made her consider another point of view and let Nathan have his say, a tormenting inner voice nagged at her, as the insidious seeds of doubt Nathan had sown in her mind began to take root.

Forcing her mind back to Will, she reflected on how often they had acted as escort for one another when they'd had to go to a hospital function, a friend's wedding or some other event. And if anyone thought they were a couple it suited them both fine not to correct them, taking the pressure off at work and socially, as neither was ready to dip their toes back into turbulent waters and try dating again.

And now Nathan had turned up in Strathlochan, determined to seek her out and stir up a hornets' nest with his talk of the past. Scared and vulnerable, Annie desperately needed Will to extend the boyfriend role for her.

'I have to keep Nathan at a distance. If he thinks you and I are together he'll leave me alone,' she explained, her worry increasing as Will shook his head again, then dragged the fingers of his free hand through his hair.

'I don't like this, Annie.'

'I know, but—'

'This isn't the best way to handle it,' Will insisted, releasing her hand and standing to pace the small room. 'I can understand it was a shock to see him again so unexpectedly, but tricking him isn't going to solve anything. At some point you are going to have to talk things over with him.'

It was her turn to rise, seeking motion to temper her inner turmoil. 'No! I can't. He hurt me, Will.' She cursed the errant tear that escaped. It hovered on her lashes for a moment before dropping on to her skin.

'I know that, and I'm sorry.' Will's smile was kind, his touch gentle as he brushed the moisture from her cheek with one finger. 'But I think you need to put things in perspective.'

'How do you mean?'

'Why are you so angry all these years on?' he countered. The question shocked her. 'You know why!'

'We all get dumped and hurt, but we pick ourselves up and go on, wiser and stronger. You've never let this go, Annie. Why is that?' His expression turned speculative as he leaned against the worktop and watched her, arms folded across his chest. 'In all the time I've know you, you've never dated anyone.'

'Pots and kettles, Will. You've been the same.'

'At first. But I don't always want to be alone, and I've started going out again. At least I'm willing to try. Are you? You use Nathan as an excuse,' he accused, and although the words were gentle they stung.

'I don't. It's just that I don't want to get hurt again. I can't trust anyone.'

'And maybe you've never got over him. Maybe you still have feelings for him…deep down inside you still love him.'

'That's ridiculous!' Her attempt to laugh off his shocking suggestion failed miserably.

'Is it? So how did you feel when you saw him again? When you heard his voice for the first time in five years? Behind your front of anger and pain, I mean,' he persisted.

'Does Nathan still make your heart miss a beat? Do your toes still curl?'

She spun away, wringing her hands together, trying to deny Will's words and the images they conjured up. 'Don't be silly. Of course not,' she denied, her pulse throbbing in her veins as she thought of her instinctive reaction when she had first looked at Nathan again, let alone his searing, erotic kiss.

'Then you have nothing to worry about, have you? You can be professional and do your job. Nathan's a good-looking guy. Olivia won't be the only one interested and in a few days he'll have women around the hospital lining up to date him.' Will's sly smile widened to a grin as he studied her face, and she tried to relax the sudden tension that had gripped her. 'You don't like that idea?'

'He's a free agent. He can see whomever he wants. He's probably dated dozens of women in the last five years.' She manufactured a casual shrug, desperate to ignore the betraying curl of despair that tightened her insides at the prospect of Nathan's hidden passions being unleashed and focused on anyone else.

'But you don't like to think of Nathan with another woman, do you?'

'Stop it!' Annie wanted to stamp her foot in angry frustration. 'Why are you doing this?'

Sighing, Will closed the gap between them and pulled her into his arms, resting his chin on top of her head. 'Oh, Annie… Why are you so scared? What do you think is going to happen if you deal with the past?'

'Nothing.' She shivered, unable to tell Will of her deep-down fear—that Nathan would ease his way back into her life and break her heart all over again.

'Don't you think you need to sort this out with Nathan once and for all?'

'No!'

'I care about you, Annie, and I'll always be here for you,' he reassured her, one hand stroking her back. 'But I think you're wrong about Nathan, and in danger of making a big mistake.'

The only danger here was Nathan himself. 'You don't know him, Will,' she protested, her voice muffled against his chest.

'No, but I saw his eyes, Annie.'

Puzzled, she drew back to look at up him. 'What are you talking about?'

'They carry the same emotions as yours, only deeper— longing and loneliness and soul deep pain.'

'Will…' Disturbed, she tried to pull away, but his hold tightened.

'Even if I agreed to do what you wanted, it's not going to solve anything,' he explained, his voice soft and patient. 'And it couldn't go on indefinitely. Nathan's going to be here for a while, and starting out with a lie is going to make things worse. At some point you are going to have to lay the past to rest—for both your sakes. You've shut it all away and it's eating at you, stopping you from living fully. Either you have to acknowledge you still care about Nathan and do something about it…or you have to let him go for good.'

Overwhelmed with tiredness and inner pain, Annie slumped against him. 'I can't do it, Will. Not at the moment, anyway. Please, play along. Give me some space to think it all out.'

A soft curse reached her ears. 'All right. A day or two. But that's *all*,' he finally conceded, with obvious reluctance.

'Thank you!' Relief washed through her as she flung her arms around him.

'Annie, I'm only doing this if you promise that you'll

think about what I said and sort things out with Nathan...
soon.'

She stepped back as Will released her, initial relief
giving way to a new uncertainty. Her feelings were
jumbled, tumultuous, disordered. She didn't want to go
back, but she was afraid to go forward. And Will's sympathetic reaction to Nathan, his insistence that she talk to the
man who once broke her heart so badly, troubled and
confused her.

'I'll think about it,' she murmured after a long pause,
knowing it was as much as she could agree to for now.

Will's face slowly changed, his eyes widening. 'I won't
have to *kiss* you, will I?' he asked with mock horror.

'Don't be gross,' she teased back, thankful that he once
again acted like the easygoing man she knew so well.

'A couple of days, Annie,' he warned a moment later,
bringing her crashing back to earth. 'Talk to Nathan.
You've been given a second chance. Don't make a mess of
it and end up with even more regrets.'

He tweaked the tip of her nose before walking out of the
kitchen, and she listened to his footsteps on the stairs as
he headed up to his bedroom. Thinking about what lay
ahead caused tension to settle like a lead weight in the pit
of her stomach. Will might have grudgingly agreed to her
little charade, but she hadn't bought herself much time. She
dreaded having to see Nathan again tomorrow as they
worked the same shift in A and E...dreaded even more that
she was not going to be able to ignore the spectre of their
past indefinitely.

'Stuart, the X-ray confirms the dislocation of your elbow,
but there is no sign of a fracture on the initial pictures,'
Nathan explained, holding the image up so that his patient,

a man in his early twenties who had fallen badly during an impromptu football game, could see the resulting injury.

'So what happens now, Doc?' Lines of anxiety and discomfort were evident on the young man's ruddy face. 'Will I need an operation?'

Nathan put the X-ray image back on the light-screen on the wall before pulling up a stool and sitting beside the trolley bed to run through the next course of action with Stuart. 'Hopefully not. We'll give you some sedation and attempt to reduce the dislocation here. If all goes to plan we'll set the arm, take another X-ray, and then you should be able to go home as soon as the sedation has worn off.'

'That sounds good. Thanks.'

'No problem.' He was satisfied that Stuart was a good candidate for the procedure, with nothing in his medical history or his current condition signifying an increased risk. Nathan turned to Gail, thankful to have an experienced nurse working with him. 'I'll need Midazolam, please, Gail,' he requested, stating the dosage.

'Of course.'

As she busied herself getting the sedative ready, Nathan told Stuart what to expect. 'The drug will be delivered intravenously,' he explained, gesturing to the cannula already inserted in the man's uninjured arm. 'Once it takes effect you'll feel drowsy, and your speech will be slurred, but you'll be able to hear me and carry out any movements I ask you to.'

'OK.'

'The sedative is ready,' Gail informed him, moving to his side.

'Thank you, Gail.' Nathan took the syringe from the nurse and double-checked it. 'Try to relax now, Stuart, and we'll have you back on your feet as soon as we can.'

Smoothly, he administered the sedative through the IV, and kept an eye on the monitors that recorded the patient's vital signs. 'While that takes effect I'll get someone to help with the reduction.'

Rising to his feet, he stepped out through the gap in the curtain. The first person he saw was Annie. His heart lurched and his pulse-rate rose—typical responses whenever he looked at her. It had been two days since he had found out about Will. Despite him having no chance to talk to her or be alone with her, the tension and electricity that shimmered between them continued to increase.

'Annie?' She spun round in surprise as he called her name, looking like a deer caught in the headlights as she noticed him. 'Do you have a moment? I need some help with a dislocated elbow.'

It was clear she was nervous as she glanced round to see if she could avoid the task, her shoulders slumping as she realised no one else was available. 'OK,' she agreed with a resigned sigh.

As she walked reluctantly towards him, Nathan reflected on how working with her was both a pain and a pleasure. Seeing Annie with Will had been as difficult as he had imagined but what he hadn't expected was to *like* the other man. He didn't want to—Will had Annie, after all. Nathan wished he could find fault with the man, but he couldn't. Aside from being a good doctor, Will had a natural way with people, and his presence brought an irreverent humour to the department, lifting the spirits of staff and patients alike and making them smile.

After his one man pity-party the evening he had been confronted with the knowledge that Annie had another man in her life, diminishing his hopes for a reconciliation with the only woman he had ever loved, he'd woken up filled with a fresh resolve. He was damned if he was going to meekly give in and let Annie go a second time. The timing might have been wrong five years ago, when he hadn't been free to pursue his own needs, but it was different now—*he* was different now—and he wasn't taking no for an answer.

For all their closeness and affection, something didn't sit right about Annie and Will. He'd thought about little else since being confronted with the information they were a couple, but he couldn't put his finger on what bothered him. Annie wasn't acting like a woman in love. She certainly hadn't been thinking of another man when she had kissed *him* with a storm of hungry, needy passion that had matched his own. Will had never been mentioned. Not until later.

No matter how she protested, Nathan didn't believe Annie was indifferent to him, or that she felt nothing. She was too skittish, too reactive. And all the while there was even a minute chance he wasn't going to stand back. It didn't help that he genuinely liked Will. The man clearly cared for Annie—but so did he. And unless he was convinced that Annie was irrevocably in love with Will, Nathan determined to persist in his efforts to lay the past to rest. If he could win Annie back in the process, so much the better. This time he was going to fight for what he wanted: the woman he needed.

Guiding Annie inside the treatment bay, he felt a quiver run through her as he rested a hand at the small of her back. She stiffened, edging away, but he had recognised the instinctive response to his touch. Forcing himself to concentrate, he briefly ran through Stuart's case.

'He's had IV Midazolam.' As Annie checked the X-rays on the screen, Nathan reassessed Stuart's condition and his level of sedation. 'Everything all right, Gail?' The nurse nodded in confirmation and smiled at him. 'OK. Stuart, we're going to sort out this elbow now.'

As Nathan flexed the elbow, Annie provided countertraction on the upper arm. Gail held Stuart's other hand, soothing him as he groaned in response to the activity, but the sedation would alleviate any recollection of the procedure once they were finished. Gently Nathan pulled on the forearm, careful not to cause any soft tissue or other damage. After a few moments the sound of a characteristic 'clunk' confirmed that the reduction had been successful and that the elbow joint had settled back into its rightful position.

'Well done.'

Annie's soft words of congratulation had him looking up. He could drown in those blue eyes. Right now a welter of conflicting emotions chased across them, and several silent moments passed between them before Annie blinked and stepped back.

'It's all in the technique,' he murmured, seeing the faint wash of colour stain her cheeks.

He hadn't meant anything by the comment, but judging by her reaction Annie's mind had wandered—and if the heat in her eyes was anything to go by she was remembering how she had teased him when they had first made love. Sated and boneless with satisfaction, she'd smiled in surprise and pleasure and joked about never imagining his intensity inside, given his outer reserve. He couldn't stop the slow smile that curved his mouth at the memory, and her blush deepened further. Hell, no, Annie hadn't forgotten—and she wasn't as indifferent as she wanted him to believe.

Remembering where they were, Nathan reluctantly broke the spell of the moment and returned his focus to his patient. 'We're done now, Stuart. The elbow is back in and you'll be feeling much better soon,' he reassured him, re-checking the pulses in the injured arm as Gail made the young man as comfortable as possible.

'Would you like me to arrange for the other X-ray?' the kindly nurse asked.

'Yes, please. I want to ensure there's no ensuing or hidden fracture. We'll get a plaster of Paris backslab on first, though, Gail,' he decreed, writing up the notes. 'And keep a close eye on him for any after-effects from the sedation. Does he have family?'

'Yes,' Gail confirmed, after a quick glance at her paperwork. 'He lives with his fiancée. She's at work, and he didn't want me to ring her until he knew what was happening.'

Nathan handed her his notes for the file and put his pen back in his pocket. 'OK. I'll check back on him in a while, when he's more alert. When he's well enough I'll write him up some medication and he can go home with supervision. Thanks, Gail.'

'My pleasure.' She gave him a motherly smile, her gaze curious as she looked from him to Annie. 'I'll phone Stuart's fiancée now.'

Leaving the cubicle and walking back to Reception with Annie, Nathan rested a hand on her arm, detaining her in a quiet corner. Her warm skin was super-soft beneath his fingertips. Again she edged away from his touch, but not before he experienced the heat of the contact searing his flesh, and felt the shiver that rippled through her. He hated the awkwardness between them, but was not about to let her coolness put him off.

'Thank you, too, for your help in there.'

'It's my job,' she pointed out with a casual shrug, crossing her arms and looking away from him.

Nathan wasn't deceived by her dismissive tone. 'We still need to talk, Annie. I'm not giving up.'

'Nathan, I—' Her nervous words were cut off as someone called to them, and, while he was frustrated at yet another interruption, Annie was visibly relieved.

'Two doctors—just what I need!' The sister in charge approached, a determined gleam in her eyes. 'We have two patients on the way in with smoke inhalation. Firefighters pulled them out of a burning workshop. No further details as yet.'

Realising he was not going to pin Annie down now to a time and place to talk, Nathan sighed, took the sparse file the sister handed him, and set off for the ambulance bay to meet the patient assigned to him. As the vehicle drew up Annie joined him, keeping what she clearly thought was a safe distance between them. The doors opened and it became apparent that both their patients were aboard. Before moving forward to assist, Nathan stepped in front of Annie, forcing her to look at him.

'Soon,' he promised, trailing the tip of one finger down the smoothness of her cheek.

By the time she had finished dealing with the young man who had suffered smoke inhalation—battling to find him a bed in already full wards, as he needed to be admitted for further observation—Annie was still unable to put Nathan's dictate out of her mind. More worryingly, her skin continued to tingle from the gentle brush of his finger.

What was she going to do? She was no closer to making a decision than she had been a couple of days ago, when his reappearance in her life had first driven her to her knees in shock. Even sticking to Will like glue had failed to give her the respite she had hoped for. Nathan was everywhere, and the sight of him, the sound of his voice, his every casual touch, all combined to heighten her unwanted desire for him, driving her insane with doubt and anxiety as well as flooding her mind with unbidden memories of their four years together.

She had thought Nathan would back off once he realised she was seeing someone else, but he had been far more tenacious than she had expected. All of which left her in an agony of indecision, living on a razor-edge of tension and emotion. She was desperate to escape Nathan's proximity. His heated looks, whispered words and teasing touches fired her blood, leaving her restless and short of breath. She was looking forward to some respite, thankful that they both had the next couple of days off before being scheduled together for three late shifts.

'One more for you, Annie,' the receptionist told her when she handed over the notes she had just completed. 'A firefighter hurt in the workshop incident.'

'Thanks.'

Annie took the notes and went through to the waiting area, having no trouble in locating her patient amongst the clusters of people taking their turn to be seen.

'Anthony Milligan?' she called, smiling as the good-looking man in uniform rose to his feet.

He had soot smudges marking his cheeks and jaw, his jacket had been discarded, his fire service T-shirt was torn, and one forearm was wrapped in a makeshift bloodied bandage. Dark-haired and hazel-eyed, Annie judged him to be in his late twenties or early thirties. He could have stepped off the pages of a firefighters calendar, she decided, noting the way all female gazes followed his progress as she led him towards the treatment cubicles. She didn't recognise him, and soon discovered he had only just joined the local crew, having recently moved to Strathlochan on promotion.

They chatted as Annie pulled on her gloves and drew up a stool so she could move in closer to study the wound on his arm. 'This looks nasty,' she sympathized, once she had removed the dressing and started to examine the deep, jagged cut that ran several inches between his wrist and his elbow.

'A canister exploded in the workshop and I was caught by some flying debris.'

Collecting the items she needed, she set about cleaning the area, laughing at Anthony's teasing comments as she worked.

'Are you trying to chat me up?' she teased.

'Sorry.' Unrepentant, his hazel eyes twinkled with amusement. 'I might try it if I wasn't gay.'

After giving him some local anaesthetic, Annie sat back and looked at him thoughtfully. 'And are you seeing anyone?'

'Not at the moment. Like I said, I've just moved here and I don't know anyone yet.'

'Really?'

'Mmm. There was someone a while ago, but...' He paused, and she sensed lingering hurt inside him before he smiled again. 'Well, things didn't work out.'

Annie took off her gloves and tossed them in the bin, a plan forming in her mind. 'Maybe you've come to the right place, then.'

'How so?'

'Don't you worry.' She peeped out of the curtain and turned back to him with a wink. 'I'm going to find someone to stitch that cut for you.'

It only took her a few moments to track Will down to the staffroom, where he was snatching a rare break. Unfortunately Nathan was there, too. His presence gave her pause—it was a complication she could have done without.

How was she going to alert Will without giving any hint to Nathan that her relationship with Will wasn't genuine? One way was to keep things light and jokey, and she could resort to a code that Nathan wouldn't understand.

Her mind made up, she tried to ignore Nathan as she walked across to join Will, but she felt him watching her the whole time and a ripple of awareness ran along her spine.

Nathan finished his mug of tea, his gaze on Annie as she sidled across to Will. She was up to something. He knew that mischievous expression of old, and trouble usually followed in its wake.

'I've just met Strathlochan's hunky new firefighter,' she announced with a provocative smile.

Will looked up from the medical magazine he was flicking through and raised an eyebrow in query. 'How hunky?'

'GAG hunky.'

What the hell did GAG mean? Nathan frowned, noting the interested speculation that sparked in Will's grey eyes as he tossed the magazine aside.

'He got a nasty cut during that workshop incident earlier,' Annie continued, her smile widening. 'I've given him a local anaesthetic, and I'm just waiting for that to work before going back to stitch his arm.'

'I'll do it for you, hon,' Will announced, rising to his feet.

'I thought you might.' Annie chuckled as Will passed her on his way to the door. 'Cubicle Three.'

'What was that about?' Nathan's puzzlement bettered him, and the question escaped before he could prevent it.

'Nothing.'

Annie's frosty reply had his frown deepening. There had been undercurrents he hadn't understood—silent messages passing between Annie and Will. Why had Will wanted to take over the stitching? Was he jealous, or worried that Annie was attracted to this 'hunky' firefighter?

Before he could ask anything more, or take the chance of having some private time with Annie, the door opened and one of the nurses peeped in. 'Sorry to disturb your break—we get few enough of them—but minors is filling up again, and Sister is on the rampage. The other doctors are busy with patients, and Robert is in Resus with a young woman with a suspected ectopic pregnancy. Can you come?'

'Of course,' he and Annie agreed in unison.

Cursing the loss of another opportunity to speak to Annie alone, Nathan followed her back to the department. Even the customary scrubs couldn't detract from the graceful way she moved—the sexy sway of her hips, her innate femininity. The shapeless material hid a body that made his mouth water…toned muscle, womanly curves and impossibly silky-soft skin. He couldn't bear to believe that he would never see or touch her again—that it had been five long years since they had made love and been consumed by a fire of passion that had raged hotter and hotter between them.

More than anything he wanted to sweep her into his arms, carry her off somewhere private and never let her go again. The temptation to do so was great. Will or no Will. And, whilst he'd never had caveman tendencies before, if Annie found ways to avoid him for much longer he might just have to act out of sheer desperation. Then, after he'd loved her into oblivion and sated the desire that burned within him, he would somehow make her listen—make her face up to the mistakes they had both made in the past. He didn't absolve himself, but Annie had to accept the truth of her own responsibility, and at the moment she wasn't doing that.

So desperate was he to spend time with her that he had even agreed to fill a gap in the department's ten-pin bowling team that evening. He was uneasy in social situations but, having discovered Annie was on the team, he was prepared to do whatever was necessary to keep in her sight and her thoughts. Even if it meant being with other people, who made him uncomfortable.

Frustrated at the way Annie was ignoring him, edgy and uncertain about where things might go between them, he took the file handed to him at Reception and went in search of his next patient. It turned out to be a quick and simple case to solve. A teenage girl, who had just begun to use contact lenses, had experienced difficulty removing one, causing her to panic and make her eye sore. Under the watchful gaze of the girl's father, Nathan moistened the displaced soft lens with saline, and was then able to remove the offending object without too much problem. After giving her advice on how to bathe her eye, and guidance on how to use her lenses, he showed her and her father out.

Nathan returned to the desk to sign off his case and collect the information for his next patient just as Will pulled back the curtain around Cubicle Three and escorted the injured firefighter towards Reception. Nathan looked the man over. He supposed he was attractive, in the rugged pin-up sort of way that appealed to women. Will shook the man's hand and moved to wipe his details off the main whiteboard, signifying the treatment cubicle was free. Nathan was about to turn away when Annie appeared out of nowhere and hurried towards the exit after the departing firefighter.

'She wouldn't...' Will groaned.

Standing beside him, Nathan watched as Annie put her hand on the firefighter's arm, talking and laughing with him. They both looked round, glancing towards Will and himself, and then the firefighter was writing something on a piece of paper Annie gave him, smiling as he tucked it in the pocket of her scrubs. With that he turned and left.

'Damn it, Annie, what have you done?' Will demanded as Annie walked back to them, giving a saucy wink as she approached.

'Anthony doesn't know anyone here. So I've got his number and said we'd be happy to help him settle in.' Unrepentant, she grinned. 'He's coming to the get-together tonight—and I've invited him round for dinner next week.'

Stunned at the way Annie was all but taunting Will, having flirted with another man right in front of him, Nathan felt his concern and puzzlement increase. The Annie he had known five years ago would never have done such a thing. Had she changed that much? She had kissed him, after all, while being involved with Will. A knot of disappointment tightened inside him.

Will advanced towards her. 'Are you going to give me that piece of paper?'

'I haven't decided!'

'I'll have to spank you if you don't behave,' Will warned, but Annie just laughed and kissed his cheek.

'Promises, promises!' Picking up a patient file, she headed to the waiting room, glancing back over her shoulder. 'Be nice to me and who knows what I'll do for you?'

Nathan had tensed at the very idea of Will spanking Annie, even if she thought it was funny. He turned to remonstrate, expecting to find anger on the other man's face, but Will was laughing.

'She's amazing, isn't she?'

'Amazing,' Nathan murmured.

As Will took the next file out of the tray and went to call

his own patient, Nathan shook his head, totally bemused. What on earth was going on between those two? He was determined to find out. Because there was something very odd that he was missing, and if all was not well between the couple he needed to know. If there was the vaguest chance that he could win Annie back, he planned on doing it.

Somehow he was going to get Annie alone, sort out the past, unravel the present, and see if there was any way they could still have a future together.

CHAPTER FIVE

'ARE you ready to go, hon? We're going to be late.'

'I'll be there in a minute,' Annie called down the stairs, in response to Will's query.

The evening she had been so looking forward to—meeting up with friends, relaxing and having fun—had become an ordeal to be faced now she had learned that Nathan had been cajoled into filling the empty space on the A and E department's ten-pin bowling team. Spending time with him, albeit in the company of others, was not a good idea. Not given how horribly aware she was of him, and how her body betrayed her at the slightest provocation. While her mind rebelled, filled with hurt and fear and confusion, urging her to keep Nathan at a distance, every cell and hormone within her came surging to life around him and demanded she rip his clothes off and have her way with him.

No way was she going to do *that*, she assured herself. She wasn't. She couldn't afford the pain of repeating the past. So why was she still in front of the mirror, fussing with her appearance in a way she hadn't bothered doing for years? an annoying inner voice taunted her. She refused to admit that she had taken extra care to look nice because of Nathan. Disconcerted, she set down her hairbrush, dabbed her pulse-points with her favourite jasmine scent and walked out of the room, determined to set Nathan from her mind.

Only his image refused to be banished. She saw him as she had first known him, reserved and alone, and as he was now, more mature, just as attractive and sexy, but still with that aloof, unapproachable air. She saw him as he was in his doctor role, caring and attentive, incredibly gentle and sweet with children, respectful and kind to the elderly, stalwart and ice-cool in an emergency. She could see his rare smile, see the way the shutters sometimes came down to hide his emotions, see that heated, sensual look that darkened his eyes when he looked at her. She shivered in response to the memory of that look.

Then she nearly laughed out loud as she recalled the utter confusion that had been on his face that afternoon when she had accosted Anthony Milligan, the new fire-fighter, and got his phone number before he had left the hospital. She could only imagine what Nathan had thought. It was clear he had no clue what had happened, and hadn't deciphered the code she and Will used.

Her smile faded as she jogged down the stairs and followed Will outside into the chilly night air. It had seemed such a good plan at the time. She really liked Anthony. He was smart and funny, and it was clear he and Will had hit it off. She had been so pleased with herself that the implications of her matchmaking had taken a while to sink in. Only while enjoying a hot shower before preparing for the evening out had she realised that if she succeeded in getting Will and Anthony together it was going to seriously affect her own situation. She needed Will as a diversion against Nathan, but she also wanted Will to be happy. He deserved it, and had been on his own too long after his painful break-up with that creep Carl. Anthony could be just what he needed—and vice versa, she thought, remembering Anthony's own story.

Sitting in silence in the car, on the way to the sports and entertainment complex that housed the ten-pin bowling lanes, Annie worried her lower lip with her teeth. If she wasn't very careful things were going to get impossibly complicated.

The truth of that was driven home to her as the evening progressed. The usual crowd of assorted medical staff, fire and rescue personnel and police officers had assembled for their monthly gathering. Noisy, irreverent and exuberant, they mingled and chatted over vast quantities of pizza, beer and soft drinks, whilst taking turns on the bowling lanes, each four-person team determined to win for their unit or department.

Trying to avoid Nathan, Annie first sat with her friend Gina McNaught. One of the best trauma nurses Annie had worked with, Gina had left the hospital a few months ago to join the staff at the town's new multi-purpose drop-in centre. It was Gina's defection from the A and E bowling team that had left a spot open for Nathan to fill tonight. After spending some time with Gina, and hearing all about her upcoming wedding, planned for May, Annie arranged to meet up with her to go swimming and have lunch on the next day they were both off duty. She swiftly moved on when she spotted Nathan closing in on her.

Annie managed to escape only because he had been waylaid by Olivia Barr. Watching the nurse flirt shamelessly with Nathan made her uncomfortable, and she experienced deep satisfaction at the way Nathan evaded the predatory woman. Another sign of her contrariness. Annie sighed, confused at her wayward emotions. She didn't want to feel anything, but she couldn't stop her warm, fuzzy relief at Nathan's obvious uninterest in Olivia, who flounced away in her high heels and impossibly short skirt, a disgruntled pout on her furious face.

And now Nathan was deep in conversation with two of the drop-in centre's doctors: Seb Adriani, Gina's handsome Italian fiancé, and Thornton Gallagher, the enigmatic clinical director. At that moment Nathan glanced up and met her gaze. There was a promise—or a threat—in his dark eyes, one that matched his earlier one-word declaration...'*soon*'. It warned her that, however much she tried to hide in plain sight, she was not going to evade and deny him for long. The sensual hunger he made no effort to mask caused a slow-burn heat to warm her from the inside out, trapping the breath in her lungs and tightening the hollow ache in her womb. How could he still affect her so intensely after all the heartache he had caused her? Did she have no sense of self-preservation?

Annie set down her drink when she realised her hands were shaking. If only Nathan had never come to Strathlochan. Exactly why he had, and why he was so determined to pursue things with her now, she was too scared to examine. Far better that she kept her distance. She couldn't allow him close again. The pain had been so terrible last time that she knew she would never survive a second experience. He hadn't cared for her enough before—had rejected her, refused to commit—so why did he want her now? What was the purpose in raking over dead ground and opening old wounds after all this time?

'So, what's the story with you and Nathan?'

'Mmm?'

Callie's voice had penetrated Annie's troubled reverie, and she pulled her gaze away from Nathan's compelling, almost psychic hold with difficulty and turned towards the woman who sat next to her. Callie was positively glowing—unsurprising, as not only was married life clearly agreeing with her, but she had just confided that she was pregnant.

'Sorry. What did you say?'

'You and Nathan?' her friend persisted.

Annie felt warmth heat her cheeks, and she looked towards the lanes as Callie's husband, Frazer McInnes, a flight doctor with the local air ambulance, sent his ball down for a perfect strike, earning a high five from his teammates and a delighted cheer from Callie.

'There is *no* me and Nathan.' Her delayed protest sounded awkward to her own ears.

'Right.' Callie's chuckle was laden with disbelief. 'You've been watching him all evening like a starved chocoholic let loose amongst the pick-and-mix.'

'I have not!'

Callie waved her objection aside. 'You have so. I thought you were going to claw Olivia's eyes out when she turned the full force of her questionable charms on him. Not that he was remotely interested.'

'We were together in med school,' Annie admitted after a moment's pause, lowering her voice.

Her friend's unusual purple-hued eyes widened with surprise and curiosity. 'Together as in *together*? Oh, my!'

'What?'

'Come on, Annie. In all the time I've known you, you've never so much as talked about a man. And you always refuse to date. Is Nathan the reason for that?'

Annie sighed, alarmed at her friend's perception. 'It's complicated.'

'I have time.' Callie smiled and gave her a gentle nudge.

'Just as you had time for me when I first came here two Christmases ago. I'll never forget all you did for me, Annie, or the way you took me under your wing. My first ever friend.'

A lump formed in Annie's throat as she remembered the old Callie, the one who had been so cut off, so defensive and tough, recovering alone from a frightening scare with pre-cancer that had seen the young woman lose part of one breast. Callie was in full health again now, contented and happy, and planning to give up her role as flight paramedic on the helicopter during her pregnancy.

Annie liked to think she'd played a small part in helping Frazer and Callie get together. Now, seeing their love grow stronger by the day, Annie felt an unwelcome and unwanted surge of envy—just as she had at their Christmas Eve wedding. She had tricked herself into believing she'd had a lucky escape with Nathan, that it would never have worked if he *had* married her as she had wanted, but deep inside she didn't believe it.

Against her will she found herself turning to look at Nathan again, her heart clenching as she drank in his chiselled good looks, reading clearly his tension and discomfort in this social setting. Parts of him she knew so well; parts she didn't know at all. The pain of being separated from him was acute. The rush of regret hit her out of the blue, swamping her. She feared she had lost something important, someone special, a vital part of herself.

She had changed a lot in the last five years. It was a shock to think back and make herself take a fresh look at that terrible last day. They had never argued before. Not in over four years of living together, or before that during their months of friendship. Somehow, in an instant, it had all blown up and raged out of control. Now Nathan accused her of never giving him a chance, of forcing his hand and refusing to listen to his point of view. She hated to admit it, but she feared there might be some truth in what he said. A truth she didn't want to examine too closely.

She had buried their row so deeply that the details were a blur. It had been the only way she could survive. If she was honest with herself, she could believe that some of the responsibility for the way things had ended *did* rest with her. But even acknowledging that didn't dull the hurt of Nathan's rejection. Or help her come to a decision about what to do now. She didn't want to open the sealed vault in which she had enclosed those hurtful memories, scared of what she would find. And what purpose would talking it all over serve for either of them five years on?

From beneath her lashes she watched as Nathan moved away from the drop-in centre staff and joined matronly A and E nurse Gail and her husband. A frown creased Annie's brow as she noticed the direction of Nathan's gaze. He was watching Will and Anthony, who were laughing together and arguing good-naturedly over the fire service's disputed bowling score. Nathan couldn't suspect anything, could he? Alarm skittered along her nerve-endings. It was too soon to have her cover plan blown apart. She was nowhere near ready to make a decision on what to do about Nathan.

'What happened between you two?'

Callie's softly voiced question sent a swift dart of pain straight to her heart. 'Nathan didn't want to make a commitment. I did.'

'Did he tell you why?' Callie pressed, forcing Annie to examine things she found too uncomfortable to deal with.

'No—' She broke off, unable to say more, weighed down by the rush of confused memories and feelings that threatened to overwhelm her. 'Until the other day I'd not seen or spoken to him in five years.'

'You still love him.'

Her friend's statement had panicked denial clamouring for freedom. Clenching her hands into fists, Annie shook her head but bit the words back, too uncertain and scared about her mixed emotions, about the thoughts and images from the past that had begun to challenge all she had once believed since Nathan's rejection of her.

'I can't,' she whispered, her traitorous gaze once more resting on him as he turned his attention from Will back to Gail and her husband, listening attentively to what they were saying. Just looking at him still had an overpowering effect on her. 'It hurt too much, Callie.'

'You are so good at caring for other people, whether it's your patients or your friends. You're always so giving and funny and alive. But maybe this is the time to think about yourself for once, and go after what you want. Annie, you deserve happiness and love, too.'

'I don't know. I'm contented with my work and my friends, Callie. Since seeing Nathan again—' She broke off, running a hand through her hair. 'I'm so confused.'

'Annie, your advice when I came here made me realise that I couldn't live in the past or let it rule the rest of my life—that sometimes we have to take a risk to win the prize. You were right. I faced the fear, leaped off the precipice, and Frazer caught me. I'm happier than I've ever been in my life.' Callie paused a moment and bit her lip, her eyes full of concern. 'Don't you think you should do the same?'

Annie opened her mouth to say no, to voice the pain and resentment that still clenched inside her, to protest that Nathan had *rejected* her, *wounded* her, hadn't loved her, but the words wouldn't come. Doubt assailed her as the uncomfortable knowledge that maybe it hadn't all been Nathan's fault tormented her. She had blamed him for so long, had used her anger and hurt as a shield against him and the rest of the world as her only means to cope, to go on, blanking out many of the details. In consequence, had she at best embroidered the truth, at worst altered reality?

'I've only just met Nathan tonight, but I've seen the way you've been looking at each other. An almost electric connection shimmers between you two. It's obvious how he feels about you. And you about him. You're both hurting, stubborn, anxious. But you have a second chance, Annie. If Nathan means anything to you, don't waste it,' Callie finished, echoing Will's words from the other day.

As Frazer hit another strike, winning the evening's competition for the air ambulance crew over the fire service team, Callie raced across to fling herself into her husband's arms and give him a congratulatory kiss. Annie watched them, happy for them and yet envious, too, aware of the black hole inside her that nothing seemed to fill.

Her thoughts and emotions disturbed her. And she had no answers to the endless questions plaguing her, leaving her feeling torn in two and impossibly confused. The idea that she might never have got over Nathan was frightening, giving the lie to her so-called recovery. Quite why the prospect of talking to Nathan made her so afraid she couldn't put into words. She just knew that the very idea of remembering those terrible last moments with him made her recoil, a tight knot of ice-cold anxiety clenching inside her. Not to mention the way she remained so vulnerable and open to more hurt.

And she was all too aware that almost from the first moment she had seen him again—certainly from the time she had run from their explosive kiss in panic—she had been lying to him. That was hardly a good basis for renewing any kind of…what? Friendship? Relationship? Just what *did* Nathan want?

'The stupidity of people never ceases to amaze me.'

Silently agreeing with Will's comment, Nathan sank into an old but comfortable armchair in the staffroom. 'The "it-will-never-happen-to-me" syndrome,' he murmured, cupping a mug of hot tea in his hands.

'Ain't that the truth?' Will agreed with a grimace.

'Well, the idea that a group of parents would take young teenagers up into the hills in this weather, with so little preparation, protection or planning, makes me furious,' Gail grumbled, her customary calm flustered by the events of the morning. 'Thanks,' she added, accepting the tea Will offered her and taking a couple of cookies from the tin before sitting on the three-seater sofa. 'I need this. Then I'm out of here—and not a moment too soon.'

Nathan couldn't agree more. After a hectic run of three night shifts, he was looking forward to some down time. Since the ten-pin bowling evening he had still not managed to talk to Annie. Despite his dislike of social gatherings, he had enjoyed the get-together—partly because he had talked with some of Annie's friends and learned more about her life in Strathlochan. Five years of her life he had un-willingly missed out on.

He had also enjoyed meeting Thornton Gallagher and the other staff from the drop-in centre, and he'd followed up an invitation to spend part of the time on his days off looking round the place. He'd been impressed with what they were doing there, and were he to stay for any length of time in Strathlochan he would definitely volunteer there.

Despite his visit to the centre, and spending hours reading and studying to increase his medical knowledge and prepare for making up to specialist registrar status, the time had dragged before he could return to the hospital and see Annie again. Her avoidance tactics were wearing his patience thin. And the bone-deep weariness from this last shift wasn't helping, he admitted, knowing the events of the last hours had made everyone short-tempered.

With a tired sigh, Will sat next to Gail and took a long drink from his own mug. Only the three of them were left in the staffroom. Nathan was lingering out of pure stubbornness, determined to wait for Annie—to wait *out* Annie. Which seemed to be his lot in life this last week. Leaning back, he closed his eyes, allowing Will and Gail's conversation to drift around him.

Work had been the only thing that had kept him busy and his mind off his troubles. And this morning had been manic, making them all late leaving. Reports had begun to come in the early hours about a party missing overnight on the hills. The mountain rescue team, complete with a couple of search-and-rescue dogs, had been out for ages in atrocious conditions—biting winds, snow and freezing temperatures—attempting to find them. There had been no proper notification of the route the party had planned to take, and, once finally found, their lack of equipment, protective clothing and common sense had baffled everyone. They had also split into three small groups, which had complicated the search further.

Once they had been located it had taken time to bring them safely off the hills. The most seriously injured had been air-lifted by helicopter—precarious in the conditions—while the rest had been ferried to Strathlochan by a small fleet of road ambulances. The A and E department had been on full alert to receive them, and everyone had worked hard to cope with the influx. Several adults and young teenagers had suffered moderate hypothermia and had required careful attention, investigation and rewarming to raise their core body temperature. A couple of the party had fallen—one adult male had nasty fractures to both arms and an ankle, one young woman had broken ribs and a punctured lung, and a teenage boy had shoulder injuries.

Nathan looked up as the door opened and Annie came in. He couldn't stop watching her. And he couldn't fail to note the fatigue on her face, the dark shadows under her blue eyes. To him she still looked stunning, and his whole being filled with the inevitable mix of love and longing, pain and uncertainty. Her gaze met his, and for an endless moment they stared at each other. It was as if the room faded away and no one existed but them. Then Annie bit her lip, her movements jerky as she moved to the counter and busied herself making a hot drink.

'All finished out there, Annie?' Gail asked, finishing her tea.

'With the hill walkers.' Nathan heard the tension and tiredness in Annie's voice as she answered. 'Robert is with a serious accident victim in Resus, and minors is filling up again. Thank goodness it's not our problem and the next shift have taken over.'

Gail rose to her feet and crossed to the sink to wash her mug. 'Amen to that. I'm away, then. I'll see you all in three days. Enjoy your time off.'

They said their goodbyes, and after Gail had left Nathan returned his attention to Annie.

'How's the boy with shoulder injuries?' he asked, as much to keep her talking as anything else.

Turning, she leaned against the counter and sipped her coffee. 'He has a grade three acromio-clavicular injury. The ligaments have ruptured and the joint was dislocated. I've referred him for possible internal fixation.'

As she spoke, she walked across to join Will. Nathan's gut clenched and his throat tightened as she attempted to snuggle up on the other man's lap, but he was puzzled when Will looked uncomfortable, throwing her a speaking look as he shifted her from him and on to her own seat on the sofa. Alert to everything about Annie, Nathan couldn't help but wonder if something was wrong. And, while he didn't want her hurt, everything in him urged that he stake his claim.

At that moment the door opened and Holly stepped inside. The young nurse looked even sadder than usual, her face pale, her eyes almost haunted, and Nathan's concern for her increased.

'Annie, can I have a quick word?' she asked with a wobbly smile.

'Of course.'

As Annie rose and moved towards the door, Nathan couldn't help but follow her every step, his gaze lingering on her until she disappeared from view. Silence stretched for a few moments. When Nathan refocused his attention, it was to find Will watching him, a speculative glint in his eyes.

'You're still in love with Annie.' The statement was made with candour, but no hint of confrontation.

'Yes,' Nathan agreed, deciding to be equally up-front and straightforward, so that there were no misunderstandings about his intentions. 'I came to Strathlochan because I needed to find Annie and deal with the past.'

A small smile played at Will's mouth. 'And to win her back?'

'As soon as I saw her again I knew the chemistry and the feelings were still as strong as ever. I can't walk away.'

'I've seen a photo of the two of you—you looked good together,' Will admitted, surprising him.

'The only time in my life I've known happiness was when I was with Annie.'

Will drained his mug and set it aside. 'So why did you dump her?'

'Is that what Annie told you?' New pain piled on top of old hurts. 'I didn't dump her, Will. I never wanted her to go—never stopped loving her. Annie left me.'

'She did? Why?'

Frowning, he tried to mask his emotions. Discussing this with Will made him uncomfortable, and he was confused at the other man's manner. 'I think you should ask Annie that.'

'I will.' This time Will's smile held sympathy.

'I made mistakes. I don't deny that.' Nathan paused, dragging his fingers through his hair, his agitation increasing. 'But Annie's formed her own reality of the past. I'd hoped by this time that we could at least talk, that she could acknowledge her part in what happened, but she refuses to listen, to discuss anything.'

There was no triumph in Will's expression, just understanding. It made Nathan feel worse. That the man Annie was now involved with saw his pain and knew how he loved her, even felt sorry for him, was hard to bear.

'Hang in there, mate,' Will advised.

Nathan's frown deepened, and he tried to read the expression in the other man's grey eyes. 'Sorry?'

'Things are not always as they seem.' Will winked before rising to his feet and crossing to switch the kettle back on. 'Do you want another cuppa?'

'No, thanks.'

He watched in bewilderment as Will fixed himself more tea. He'd never been as confused in his life as he had this last week. What did Will mean? That he might give Annie up? But Will professed to love her, and she loved him, so what was going on here? Nothing made sense any more.

Before he could gather his thoughts, Annie returned, followed by Holly, who had changed out of her uniform and was ready to go home.

'I just stopped in to say goodbye,' she said with a fractured smile, nodding at Annie, who gave her a quick hug. 'Well, not goodbye, as such. But this was my last shift in A and E. I'm moving up to the children's ward.'

A moment of silence greeted her announcement, then Will found his voice. 'Are you sure, Holly?'

'Yes. I need to do this. It's been great working with you all. And I'll still be around,' she added, forcing another unconvincing smile.

When Holly had gone, Nathan turned to the others in surprise. 'Did you know she was planning this?'

'No.' Will's usually smiling face was sombre. 'It's a real shame… and the department is losing a great nurse.'

Nathan couldn't agree more. He had enjoyed working with Holly, and found her to be skilled, compassionate and eager to learn.

'It's too hard on her to be around Gus all the time,' Annie explained, sitting back down on the sofa.

Cradling his second mug of tea, Will leaned against the counter, his legs crossed at the ankles. 'Holly really cares about Gus. I'm not sure what happened, but they were attracted to each other when Gus first came here in the summer. They were going to go out, but there was some misunderstanding, and Holly's sister Julia stepped in and ensnared him.'

'Ensnared?' Nathan queried.

'Julia makes Olivia seem like Mother Teresa,' Annie

filled in, her tone derisive. 'She's done this to Holly before, and is a real bitch to her.'

Will nodded, taking up the story again. 'This time Julia managed to *marry* the man Holly wanted.'

'Only because she trapped him by getting pregnant without his knowledge. He did the decent thing, but Julia doesn't give a damn about Gus...and you can see how miserable they all are. I just don't understand how Julia could *do* such a thing,' Annie raged, her disgust and indignation evident.

Nathan felt as if all the air had been sucked out of his lungs. As sympathetic as he was for Holly's situation, it was his own remembered pain and confusion that was uppermost in his mind once more. Aware of the quiet in the room, he stood up, his gaze focused on Annie, on the puzzlement in her face as she looked at him. Could she *really* not know? Had she buried her memories so deep that the irony just didn't occur to her?

'Don't you, Annie?' he asked, keeping his voice deceptively soft, managing to mask the sudden anger licking through him if not the welling of hurt. 'I would have thought you'd understand perfectly. It's what you planned to do to me, after all.'

CHAPTER SIX

SHE was a coward. That was the only explanation, Annie admitted, as she lay alone in the dark bedroom at her old family home in Yorkshire, listening to the wind rattle the roof slates and the darts of rain dash against the window. She had run away—again.

After Nathan's devastating bombshell, she had no longer been able to suppress the truth—the reality she had somehow managed to twist around in her mind in order to survive the full horror of what had happened five years ago and her part in it. Overwhelmed with confusion, and swamped by guilt as Nathan had walked out of the staff-room, she had been left alone with Will, who had all but marched her from the hospital and taken her home.

The conversation that had followed made her groan even now.

'Annie, you know I want to help you, but this can't go on. It was one thing pretending we were a couple for a day or two, but things are getting out of hand,' Will stated, sitting her down, his expression serious. 'How long are you going to punish Nathan? You are deliberately hurting him, and it's just not like you to be cruel. It's time to deal with it. What happened? You told me Nathan dumped you, rejected you.'

'It felt like that.' She cringed inside at the lameness of her answer, hating that she sounded so juvenile and knowing Will wouldn't let her get away with it.

'Come on, hon. Nathan wouldn't have said what he did in the staffroom if you hadn't hit a nerve with your comment about Julia.'

A flush warmed her face and she looked away, finding it hard to come to terms with her actions, shocked by the way she had so successfully blanked out her own selfish mistakes and blamed Nathan for everything. 'I felt a desperate need for security. I panicked and demanded that he marry me. I urgently wanted commitment and... God, Will, I threatened to stop taking the pill and get pregnant,' she whispered, forcing the horrible confession out into the open, ashamed it had taken Nathan's painful accusation to make her acknowledge her responsibility.

'Where did that desperation come from?' Will asked, sitting close and taking her hand in his.

'I don't know. I've never thought about it before. My father had died six months earlier...' She paused, affected even all this time later, pained to remember that her rock throughout that terrible time of grief had been Nathan. His support and understanding and care had been unwavering. And how had she repaid him? 'I was devastated. Lost.'

'Oh, Annie...'

'I loved Nathan. I told him that if he really loved me he'd agree to what I wanted.' She closed her eyes, embarrassed to even look at Will as she faced the truth she had avoided for five years. 'Nathan said it was too soon—that we couldn't get married and start a family.'

'You were just on the point of qualifying, weren't you? Surely it was better for Nathan to be honest than to take such an important step for the wrong reasons? What did he say?' Will prompted with damnable calm.

'I don't know.'

'Sorry?'

Annie bit her lip. 'I was hurt, and I saw Nathan's refusal as a rejection of me and what we had together. I left—him *and* the hospital—and I never saw him again until this week.'

'So you never gave him a chance to explain?'

'No.' The edge of censure in Will's voice had stung, even though she'd known she deserved it.

She felt guilty when she recalled Nathan's efforts to talk to her these last days—efforts she had blocked at every turn. Deep in her subconscious she must have known she was at fault and was evading dealing with it. How or why she had behaved in such a way was a mystery to her, but seeing Nathan again had made things she had buried for so long inexorably rise to the surface. Now that they had, and she could no longer ignore them, she felt even more frightened, even more uncertain about what to do.

'I think we've become too comfortable with each other,' Will had said then, his words shocking her from her troubling thoughts.

'What do you mean?'

'We're best friends, and I love you to pieces, but whilst we may have started out with the best of intentions we've let the situation drift and become convenient.' Will wrapped an arm around her shoulders and drew her close. 'I think it's time for us to re-evaluate things.'

'But—'

A finger to her lips silenced her protest. 'I'm ready to start living again, Annie. I really like Anthony and I plan to see him. But this isn't just about me. I went along with your charade at the beginning, even though it didn't feel right to me, but it's wrong. We have to stop. I think you need to deal with these issues about Nathan once and for all. It's time to move on. You have to talk to him.'

'I can't.' She shuddered at the thought of facing him, knowing she had wronged him. But it was more than that…it was the inner knowledge that she was still vulnerable to him.

'You can. You have to. He cares about you, Annie. He hides his feelings well, but I see the pain in his eyes when he looks at you and when he thinks we're together. I really like him, and I feel guilty doing this to him. You need to set the record straight.'

'Will—' She broke off, seeking the words to explain. 'I can't hurt like that again.'

He tightened his hold, dropping a kiss on the top of her head. 'I know you're scared. The fact that you are just proves how much you still care. If you were truly over him what happened five years ago would no longer matter to you. You can't blame Nathan for everything. And you can't use me to stand between you and the rest of your life. You're hurting Nathan and you're hurting yourself.'

'It doesn't change the fact that he didn't want me.'

'He said it was too soon for marriage and a family. That isn't the same thing,' Will pointed out, breaking down her defences with his arguments. 'You are different people now, Annie. Older, wiser, more settled. Maybe Nathan made a mistake. Maybe you asked for too much too soon. But you have the opportunity to make things right. Are you going to stubbornly deny yourself the possibility of real happiness because you are too frightened to take a chance and admit your own part in what went wrong?'

She had pushed away from him, confused, unsettled, unable to think. Most of all unwilling to face that much of what he had said might be true. Because if she did she'd have no defences left. If she allowed Nathan in, opened herself to caring for him, loving him, then she would be hurt all over again. Because he'd made it clear he didn't want marriage and a family, and she didn't think she would ever pick herself up from that a second time. But Will had been through the wringer, too, and he deserved his chance at happiness. She loved him too much as a friend, as the brother she had never had, to stand in his way. It wasn't fair of her to use him as her emotional shield.

'You need to think long and hard about what you want, Annie, and settle this once and for all.'

After Will had gone up to bed, telling her he had plans with Anthony during his time off, she had tried to grab a few hours' sleep for herself. Feeling unsettled and unrested, she had risen scant hours later, written a note to Will, and then driven to Yorkshire to see her mother, hoping the warmth and security of home would help to calm her.

Time and distance had done nothing to dull the effect of Will's words, which continued to ring in her ears. Annie sighed, turning over again and thumping her pillow, unable to rest as she tried to consider all that had happened in the past with an open and honest mind.

Losing her father had been the most terrible blow. They had been so close, and he had been her hero. A rural GP, his love of medicine and care for his patients had been her inspiration, and she had been determined to follow in his footsteps and to make him proud of her. He had supported her every step of the way when she had chosen emergency medicine—both her parents had. His sudden and unexpected death had devastated her. And Nathan had been there, seeing her through every moment.

Had she ever thanked him? Had she ever given him

anything back? No. All she had done was cling to him, make demands. Unaware of the tears tracking her cheeks, she recalled those terrible last moments when she had pushed and pushed him, with no conscious thought or understanding of what was driving her on…

'We can't have a baby now, Annie,' Nathan had explained patiently, sighing when she'd evaded his attempt to hug her. 'It's too soon, sweetheart. We're financially unstable and at a crucial point with our careers. We don't even know where we're going to be living when we move on to start training in our specialties.'

'I'm going to stop taking the pill.'

She felt his withdrawal from her at the threat. 'No. I won't be blackmailed, Annie.'

'I want us to get married, Nathan. I want a baby. If you really loved me…'

She buried her head under the duvet as she recalled her whingeing demands, saw again his set face, the unwavering expression in his implacable dark eyes. Nathan hadn't rejected her. He had been cautious and responsible. She could see it now, with painful clarity. And he had never said it was over—just that it was the wrong time for both of them to take the step to marriage and a family. He had been right, but at the time she had been blind to reason.

Behaving out of character, riddled with insecurities she had never experienced before, something self-destructive had snapped inside her and she had flown off the handle— accused him of not caring, of not loving her, not wanting to be with her, and she had walked out and never seen him again. Clearly she had hurt Nathan as much as she had hurt herself. God, what a mess. Was it too late to put things right? And even if it were possible how could she do it? She had dug an even bigger hole for herself by deceiving

Nathan and using Will as a shield. How could he trust her again when he found out?

As uncomfortable as it was to admit, Annie recognised that she had been selfish…so young, so unrealistic, so demanding, so insecure, planning her perfect life without considering Nathan's needs and wants. Without even understanding her own.

After a sleepless night, she went for a walk along familiar paths, instinctively taking routes she had shared often with her father. Today she had her mother's enthusiastic Springer spaniel, Todd, for company, but for once she was blind to the bare beauty of the wintry countryside around her. Filled with confusion and mixed emotions, she returned to the house and had a late lunch with her mother, knowing they needed to talk before she drove back to Scotland. She had work the next day—and she could no longer ignore Nathan and the confrontation that must inevitably come.

'Nathan turned up in Strathlochan last week,' she began, unsure of herself, and knowing her mother had disagreed with her actions five years ago, although they had never discussed it since.

'I know.'

Her mother's calm reaction shocked her rigid, and it took a moment for Annie to find her voice. 'You know? How?'

'Just because you decided to cut Nathan out of your life it didn't mean I had to. I always cared about him, and he was wonderful when your father died.' After pouring herself a glass of water and taking a sip, her mother continued. 'We've kept in touch these last five years. And he's never forgotten Christmas, my birthday or your father's anniversary.'

Annie was unable to process all her mother had said. She felt unsettled by the feelings welling within her, which ranged from anger to sadness to a sliver of ridiculous envy. How could she be so contrary? She had pushed Nathan away, refused to have contact with him or even mention his name for the last five years, so how could she begrudge or feel jealous of her mother's friendship with him?

'You told Nathan where I was?'

'No.' Her mother paused to stroke Todd, who gave up his fruitless vigil for a treat from the table and crossed to his doggy duvet by the Rayburn to curl up for a sleep. 'I had no idea Nathan had gone to Scotland until after the event. But I'm not surprised. He's at a turning point in his life and I suppose he needs to take care of the unfinished business between you. We've never discussed you, Annie,' she added gently. 'It was a kind of unspoken agreement so we didn't make things difficult for each other. I've never volunteered information and Nathan has never asked.'

Sudden and unexpected hurt ripped through her at the knowledge. 'Why didn't you tell me?'

'You told me not to, love.' Her mother sighed and shook her head. 'From the moment you left him and came home, announcing you were moving to another hospital, you were adamant that I was never to mention him. Even when he was phoning here, coming to the house, desperate to talk to you, you refused to listen. What was I supposed to do? You broke his heart, Annie. You're my daughter…I love you and I always will…but I wasn't about to abandon Nathan when he needed someone.'

Annie sat frozen, trying to make sense of it all. She had never known that Nathan had come after her. She had simply assumed he hadn't cared—another terrible error on her part. And all this time her mother and Nathan had remained friends, had shared things without her, had acted as if she didn't exist.

'I never could understand why you set Nathan up for a fall and tested him like that,' her mother continued, piling on more guilt and refusing to allow Annie to back away from the reality of her mistakes. 'What did you expect him to do, love? You tried to trap him into committing to you by threatening to get pregnant against his wishes.'

'I don't know why!' Annie cried, overwhelmed, battling back the tears that stung her eyes, unable to take any more. 'Somehow I blocked it all out. I've only just acknowledged what I did, but I can't make sense of the way I acted.'

'Annie…'

'I loved him so much, Mum, and I was scared he didn't love me back—scared I would lose him unless I tied him down, had a proper commitment.'

As her voice broke, her mother came around the table to sit next to her, placing a protective arm around her shoulders. 'He loved you, too. It was just the wrong time to even be thinking about a baby.'

'I couldn't see that then.'

How could she ever have been so foolish as to think for a second they could have coped with their pressured jobs, starting out as junior doctors, changing posts and hospitals, struggle to make ends meet and still brought a baby into the world? Why had she backed Nathan so far into a corner that he had had no option but to push back against her?

She voiced the questions aloud. 'Why, Mum? Why did I do that?'

'You were understandably rocked by your dad's death.'

The explanation mirrored her own thoughts, but it still shocked her to hear it out loud. 'But that was six months before my row with Nathan.'

'There's no time limit on grief, Annie. And it can drive us to do strange things. You weren't yourself after he died.'

Her mother's eyes held deep sadness. 'You think I don't still miss and yearn for your father five and a half years on? I know what he meant to you, how close you were—he loved you so much and he was incredibly proud of his little girl. He always thought of you that way,' she added with a smile. 'But he was my life, too. My world changed for ever, love, just as yours did.'

'Mum…' Fresh tears welled in her eyes at the thought of her mother, home alone, lost without the man who had been by her side for twenty-five years.

Her mother took her hand, her smile gentle and kind. 'I know, Annie, I understand. You have a lot of thinking to do to face the reality of the past and your own role in it. Don't judge Nathan so harshly without understanding his side of things.'

'But—'

'Talk, Annie, but listen, too,' she advised, with a mix of firmness and sympathy. 'You have another chance—don't make the same mistakes again. There's so much you never bothered to know about Nathan…his family, his child-hood, what shaped him to be the person he is. He's such a special man—but a very lonely one. He keeps so much locked inside him. You were the only person he ever let close to him or trusted with himself. And I don't think you have any clue how important you were in his life. You were his anchor, his joy. He's never recovered from losing you.'

By the time Annie left her old family home after her im-promptu visit, she felt as if she had been through an emo-tional wringer. And she knew worse was to come—because, as crazy as it seemed, she had to go to Nathan. She was compelled to do so, drawn to him, consumed with the need to see him.

Armed with his address, which her mother had given

her, she drove north towards Strathlochan. Having spent so long in denial, so long pushing him away, she now wanted to talk, to explain, to apologise…to learn about the man who still remained a mystery to her in so many ways, despite the intimacies they had shared.

Just how much *did* she know about Nathan apart from his skills as a doctor, his quiet kindness, protectiveness and his supreme ability as a lover? What did she know of his past, his hopes, his fears, his dreams? Nothing—just as he had said. Just as her mother had suggested. It shocked her that she knew nothing about his background, nor why he had come to study medicine at twenty-two, and not at a younger age like the rest of their group. She had assumed he'd had a change of mind about the career he wanted. Maybe she had assumed a lot of things. He had never talked of his home… She didn't even know if he had family somewhere. How could she have been so self-absorbed? She felt the terrible weight of guilt. She had known Nathan was reserved, a loner, and she acknowledged with shame that she had revelled in being the only one he turned to, confided in, allowed close to him. If all her mother had said was true, she had let him down terribly.

She had no one to blame but herself for the misery of the last five years. Even the achievements in her career seemed meaningless against the bleakness of her personal life. She had been so driven, so consumed by the loss of her father, shaken by the knowledge that nothing was safe and that life could change in a moment. She'd had her mother and Nathan, and she'd wanted to tie them both to her in a desperate need for security, scared to lose anyone else essential to her life, her heart, her soul.

Welcomed into her home, treated as part of their family, Nathan had been fond of her parents. Lost in her own torment, she'd never once thought that he might have been affected by her father's death, too. Nathan had been by her side throughout every moment of her heartache. He'd held her as she cried, listened to her talk for hours into the night about the man who had been her hero, her friend. Nathan, always understanding, always strong, always giving. What had she given him in return? Her throat tightened. Nothing. She had just taken. All too clearly she could see her mistakes, her selfishness. They were laid out before her, bare, exposed. She didn't like what she saw of herself, but she was no longer able to hide, to pretend that the fault was anyone's but her own.

How could she have been so juvenile, so thoughtless? And why had Nathan put up with her as long as he had? The truth of the answer made her sob aloud. Because, despite everything, he had loved her. And she had thrown it all back in his face when he wouldn't fit in with her sudden whim to have a baby. She had been so vulnerable after losing her father that she had subconsciously tried to tie Nathan to her, terrified he would leave her, too. And in pushing him, in reacting so irrationally to his answer, she had lost the very things she had been so desperate to keep. Nathan and his love.

She feared she didn't deserve either.

She had taken his reluctance to get married and have a baby at the moment she demanded as an out-and-out rejection of her—a sign he didn't care. Five years too late, she could see how wrong she had been...about everything. He had not been denying her or their love. He had simply— and quite rightly—said that it was too soon for them to have a child.

There was no escaping from the truth. She had behaved abominably. Her mother had tried to tell her but she hadn't listened. Neither had she given Nathan a chance to express his views. Not even these last ten days, when he had tried again and she had shoved him aside. Why had he waited until now to come after her? Her mother's suggestion that he was at a turning point in his life was scary. Did that mean he was ready to move on without her? She had wasted five years, causing herself and Nathan unimaginable pain. How could he ever forgive her? He had come to Strathlochan, but did that mean he still wanted her? Or did he just need closure before walking away—for good this time?

Restless, Nathan stood at the window in the living room of the ground floor flat he had rented for his time in Strathlochan and stared out into the darkness of the night. The rain had stopped an hour or more ago, but the wind was still strong, whistling eerily around the old detached granite building, sounding mournful, matching his mood.

Sighing, he closed the curtains and returned to his chair, unable to focus on the medical study he was doing in preparation for gaining his specialist registrar status. He had been distracted ever since he had seen Annie again, but the last days had plagued him, and he was anxious that he had ruined everything. He shouldn't have confronted Annie in the staffroom like that—especially in front of Will. But when she had made her comment about the way Holly's sister had trapped Gus Buchanan he hadn't been able to help himself.

At some point the words had needed to be said. Annie had to face the reality of the past—a reality he was realising she had genuinely managed to distort to protect herself. And his challenge had caused a reaction. He had seen it in the way her face had paled and her blue eyes had grown large and shadowed. Giving her space to think and himself a chance to cool off had seemed the best idea. Now he was scared he had acted rashly, and worried that his impatience and burst of hurt anger might have driven even more of a wedge between them.

He had made some bad mistakes in the past, and maybe he hadn't learned the lessons as well as he should have. What if it was too late to have a second chance with Annie? She was the only woman he had ever loved. Ever would love. A frown knotted his brow as his thoughts turned inexorably to her and Will. He had yet to resolve what bothered him about their relationship. They were clearly very close, their affection was genuine, and yet he hadn't detected any hint of passion. That surprised him. He himself knew the full extent of the fire that smouldered within Annie. He'd experienced the joy of inflaming it, embracing the intensity of heat they had always generated, which had threatened to consume and incinerate them.

Will's unconcern at having him around also troubled him. The other man's friendly understanding and curious comments were puzzling. Nathan had made it clear he still loved Annie and wanted her back, but rather than feel challenged it was almost as if Will was on his side. How could that be? Unless Will was so secure in Annie's feelings that he knew he didn't need to worry?

The only way to find answers to his growing list of questions was to pin Annie down once and for all—no easy matter when she evaded him at every turn. Renewed determination fired within him. He would see her tomorrow at work, and somehow he would have to convince her that they could no longer put off the talk they needed to clear the air between them. Where that talk would lead, and if they would come out the other end with any hope of salvaging the special relationship they had once shared, he had no idea. He only knew that the thought of losing Annie for good terrified him.

Running one hand across his unshaven jaw, he returned his attention to his study. Never before had he experienced so much trouble concentrating on his work. Never had his single-minded determination been so tested. Even when Annie had first left him he had thrown himself into work as a way of coping with the desolation. And he'd had the responsibilities of home weighing on him, shackling him. Now he was free—free and at a crossroads. What happened with Annie would influence the course of the rest of his life. And define whether he could know happiness again or would always remain alone.

An hour later the sound of the doorbell disturbed the concentration he had fought so hard to achieve. Who on earth could that be? He'd not had much contact with the people in the two flats on the floors above him, and he hadn't established social networks with his colleagues at the hospital. Frustrated at the interruption, he left his books open on the table and walked barefoot to the door, his breath catching in his throat as he swung it open and discovered the identity of the visitor who waited on the step.

'Annie…'

Surprised, it took him a moment to let it sink in that she was real, and not some figment of his imagination. Under the glow of the porch light her face was pale, the expression in her eyes wary, and the slight tremble of her lips was evidence of her uncharacteristic nervousness. Then, as a gust of wind whipped strands of ebony hair around her face, he realised she was standing in the cold, shivering, and hadn't even put on a coat.

'Come inside before you freeze.'

He took her arm and drew her with him into the warmth

of the flat. No way was he going to let her escape now she had sought him out and he had a chance to see her alone.

Hesitantly she stepped across the threshold and allowed him to lead her to the living room. 'I've been to see Mum—' She broke off and blinked, looking unsure, almost disorientated. 'I had no idea you'd kept in touch with each other all this time.'

A mix of incomprehension, accusation, envy and hurt laced her voice. Nathan paused, unsure what to say. It had never been his intention to shut her out or deceive her, more the acknowledgement that she had not wanted to know about or to speak of him. He had cared about both her parents, had revelled in their acceptance of him, the way they had drawn him into their family and made him feel one of them. And he'd been affected by her father's death, masking his own feelings as he had focused on caring for Annie through her grief, as well as being there for Annie's mother, Eve.

When Annie had left him her mother had insisted on remaining in regular contact with him. He had been shocked, but relieved. Eve had shown no recrimination, only quiet understanding, and their friendship had continued, with Annie an unspoken shadow between them. At the time he had felt most alone and had needed wise counsel, Eve had been there. Now she knew bits about his life that no one else did, not even Annie.

Clearly the last few days had been a shock for Annie. It showed in the strain on her face and the confusion in her eyes. Not only was she being forced to face up to the events of five years ago, but she had learned of her mother's friendship with him. Concerned for Annie's well-being, and wondering what Eve might have revealed to her daughter, Nathan took a step closer, stilling when she visibly tensed, her hands knotting in agitation.

'Would you like something to drink?' he asked, reining in his impatience to discover the reason for her visit in order to set her more at ease.

'OK.'

'Hot chocolate?' He tempted her with what had always been her favourite treat—second favourite after the dough-nuts, he amended with a reminiscent ache.

'Thank you.'

Myriad questions and emotions rampaged through him as he walked towards the kitchen, hearing her soft footsteps as she followed. He was reaching into a cupboard for a saucepan when he heard the hitch in her breathing and the strangled sob she tried unsuccessfully to mask. Forgetting the pan, he turned to face her, all thought of their separation and the awkward-ness between them gone as he saw the tears shimmering on her lashes. His only need was to comfort, to protect, to care.

'Sweetheart, what is it?' His voice was husky with his own emotion. He'd never been able to bear it when she cried. Annie was always full of life and laughter, so to see her like this was rare and disturbing. The only time she had been so distraught before was when her father had died. As he wrapped his arms around her she burrowed against him, unresisting as he drew her close, her own arms lifting to slide around his waist. 'Tell me what's wrong.'

'I'm sorry. I'm so sorry. I didn't understand what I was doing. Or why.'

The words were fractured, broken, ripped from within her. Her pain tore at him. The wetness of her tears soaked through his shirt to bathe his skin, and he cradled her closer, keeping her safe, breathing in the familiar scent that mixed with the very essence of her. Whilst he hated her distress she felt so good, so right back in his arms. He allowed the fingers of one hand to slide under the fall of her hair to begin a soothing caress over the nape of her neck, marvelling anew at the softness of her skin. At last he was touching her again, holding her after five years. Five *long* years in which he hadn't been living, only existing without her.

'Shh,' he whispered, bending his head to nuzzle against her, feeling the tremors racking her body with each sob, her ragged breath as she clung to him. 'Stop, Annie, please. You're going to make yourself ill—and you're tearing me apart.'

Drawing back a fraction, he cupped her face in his hands, bending to remove the evidence of her tears with his lips and tongue, tasting the slightly salty moisture on the downy soft skin of her cheeks. Damp, spiky lashes parted and bruised blue eyes looked into his brown ones. Mere millimetres separated them.

'Nathan…'

He felt rather than heard his name as a whisper of her breath caressed his face. His chest felt tight. Her hands loosened their grip on his shirt, her fingers a hesitant touch over his back sending waves of sensation coursing through him. They were on the cusp of something momentous. They both knew it. Nathan fought to remember Will, to remind himself of how Annie had hurt him, to recall everything that remained unsettled between them. The timing was all wrong. He didn't yet know why she had come to him this evening.

But right at this moment none of that seemed to matter a damn. He couldn't think straight with Annie so close, their breaths mingling, her warmth and her scent surrounding him. He could no more stop touching her or prevent himself from kissing her than he could stop his heart beating fast and uneven beneath his ribs.

Temptation overrode his common sense.

CHAPTER SEVEN

'PLEASE—'

Nathan wasn't sure who voiced the plea, or which of them moved first to close the last of the gap between their lips…Annie or himself. Maybe it was both of them, responding instinctively to the mutual pull. He only knew that in the next moment their mouths met—open, hot and ravenously hungry. At once the flames ignited and raged between them. He had to touch her, had to take more. The needy sounds she made in her throat, familiar but too long unheard, drove him crazy, and he deepened the contact, exploring every remembered atom of her honey-sweet mouth. He welcomed her urgent participation, allowing her tongue to twine with his, duelling and teasing before he drew her back into him, stroking her, sucking on her, swallowing her moan of pleasure.

Annie sagged against him, her fingers spearing into the thickness of his hair, holding him to her. As if he was going anywhere. His own hands roved down her back to cup her rear, flexing and shaping her delicious curves as he drew her even closer, making them both aware of how hard he was for her. Teeth nipping at his lower lip, she rubbed wantonly against him, her fingers abandoning his hair so her hands could burrow between their bodies and set to work on the buttons of his shirt.

For the briefest moment a flicker of sanity tried to prevail, reminding him of Will, of all the obstacles yet to be overcome—including the fact that he didn't know Annie's motives for being here with him now. But before he could regain a fragment of control Annie had thrown herself back into the eroticism of their kiss, sliding open the material of his shirt to expose his chest, her fingers brushing against his skin. Her touch scalded him, searing his flesh, sending flares of sensation to every nerve-ending, heightening his arousal to breaking point. Any hope of discernment was lost.

Neither of them could stop the whirlwind that had overtaken them and was now carrying them along in its wake. Hands dragged at clothes, uncaring where they fell. His loosened shirt went first. Then Annie's skirt. Her hands were fumbling with his belt and the fastening of his jeans. Nathan was scarcely aware of moving, but Annie was in his arms, her legs locked around his hips, and he was all but weaving down the corridor to the bedroom, bumping against a wall and then into the doorway in his haste, cushioning her from any harm. He was focused solely on Annie…the taste of her, the scent of her, the feel of her.

They fell to the bed in a tangle of limbs, and he reluctantly released her mouth long enough to drag her jumper over her head. Annie's boots followed, and then the last of their clothes were wrenched away. Fabric ripped, then, finally, they were flesh on flesh, their bodies gliding together, exploring, relearning, eager and impatient.

Aroused beyond bearing, Nathan couldn't believe Annie was here, back in his bed, and that he was touching her, kissing her, loving her.

'It's been so long, so long. I need you so badly.'

He mouthed his refrain against her warm, satiny skin, paying homage to the rounded firmness of her breasts, drawing each erect dark rose nipple into his mouth in turn, loving the way she cried out and arched her body to seek more of his touch. Needing to feel and taste all of her at once after years of deprivation, he feasted on her, welcoming the way her hands and mouth roved over him with equal hunger.

'Hurry.' She nipped at his earlobe, soothing it with her tongue. 'We don't have much time.'

Nathan silenced Annie's words with another deep, thorough kiss. They were words he didn't want to hear or think about or examine for meaning. A distant part of him was aware that they should slow down, that they had to talk, to resolve their issues. But Annie was back with him, they had found each other again and, despite what she had just said, they had all the time in the world to reconcile the past and plan for the future. Once they had taken the edge off this desperate hunger.

There was no extinguishing the wild conflagration that had taken on a life of its own, driving every reasoned thought from his mind. Five years of need and want refused to be denied for another second. He had enough presence of mind to fumble for a condom—purchased more in hope than expectation when he had come to Strathlochan to find Annie—then they were coming together, frantic, untamed, rough, urgent in their desire, their joining.

It was like regaining home. He belonged with Annie, *in* Annie. She felt incredible...so hot, so tight, so very *right*. Made just for him. Only she made him whole. Only she brought his body alive. For a moment he paused to savour the magnitude of his feelings, then she was dragging at him, her nails leaving marks on his back, demanding more. Nathan moved, beyond thought, and Annie matched his rhythm, taking and giving, wrapping her legs higher around him until they were so deeply and tightly joined they might never be parted. As one they raced towards the precipice, hard and fast and blissfully perfect, and unimaginable pleasure built and built until he thought he would explode.

They clung together as they soared over the edge and into the endless void, spiralling, falling, spinning out of control, crying out as their pleasure crested with the force of a volcanic eruption and ecstasy took them in its thrall. Their hearts pounded in unison; their breaths were ragged, tortured. Collapsing against Annie, he wrapped his arms around her, keeping her safe and grounded, never wanting to let her go again, overwhelmed at the out of body experience they had just shared.

Annie had no idea how long it was before she could breathe again, let alone think about moving a muscle. She was too exhausted and shaken to even attempt to open her eyes. What on earth had just happened? Making love had always been amazing for them, with Nathan taking her to the stratosphere every time, but this... What they had just shared together defied description or explanation. How could she have lived without Nathan these last five years? How could she have deceived herself so thoroughly? Something about this man called to everything within her. He completed her. Made her whole. And she had stupidly wasted so much of their lives.

Just thinking about that brought to mind all that still remained unsettled and unexplained between them. She hadn't come here this evening with the intention of doing anything except talking, but events had overtaken her and she had fallen into bed with Nathan without a second thought. Now doubt and anxiety welled inside her. Once again she had acted without thinking. But Nathan only had to touch her, to kiss her, and all common sense deserted her.

What did this evening mean to him? Had it just been a spur-of-the-moment one-off thing because she was available? There was so much yet to be discussed, but the thought of how they were ever going to sort things out daunted her. She still had no idea why Nathan had come to Strathlochan to see her, or what this crossroads in his life was that her mother had mentioned. Did he plan to move on without her once the past had been laid to rest? And what of her own part in events—then and now? Owning up to her selfish mistakes scared her—as did admitting the fact that she had been lying to him since they had met up again.

A ripple of sensation flowed through her as Nathan stirred. He was resting in a position long familiar to her, his head on her abdomen, his warm breath flowing over her navel, the strands of his hair teasing the undersides of her breasts like silken ribbons. One arm was flung over her hips, the other draped across the pillow, curved around her head, his fingers in her hair. Nathan had always made her feel cherished and protected and special, but particularly so after they'd made love.

Her tummy muscles clenched in reaction as Nathan nuzzled his face against her. The rasp of stubble on his jaw across her skin was a caress that had always thrilled and excited her. He moved so that he could swirl his tongue-tip teasingly over her flesh and dip it into her navel. She didn't think she could possibly respond again so soon, but her body proved her wrong. Arousal and a fresh knot of need were curling inside her, stoking the fire of passion into an inferno once more.

'We have to talk, Annie,' he murmured, pressing kisses over her stomach and up the valley between her breasts to the hollow of her throat. 'About so many things.'

Her fears returned with a vengeance. She had come here with the intention of talking, but now she didn't want to. Didn't want all they still had to face to intrude on the magical eroticism and closeness of this moment. What if she never had another chance to be with him?

'Not now.'

Whatever happened afterwards, she wanted this evening. She drew him to her, taking his mouth with hers, determined to distract him from the questions she knew were preying on his mind. It didn't prove to be a difficult task. Nathan was immediately on the same wavelength, taking possession of the kiss until she was weak and trembling, all her other worries forgotten, and her body was tight with needy desire, craving the fulfilment that only he could bring her. He looked down at her with drowsy sensuality, his eyes darker than ever, filled with the promise of hot passion.

'You are so beautiful, Annie.' The husky roughness of his voice made her warm all over, the reverence of his words tightening her chest with emotion. 'So special.'

After the wildness they had just experienced Nathan now took his time, driving her insane with wanting as he set off on a journey of discovery, refamiliarising himself with every particle of her body. As his mouth blazed a trail of flame from her throat down to her breasts, her hands grazed over his back and the width of his shoulders, feeling the ripple of muscle under supple flesh. She loved the texture of his skin…masculine, smooth, warm. And every time she breathed in she inhaled the subtle but heady male scent of him.

A whimper escaped as the heat of his mouth captured one nipple, swollen and peaked with arousal. His teeth nipped teasingly, before his tongue salved the sensual sting. His lips closed, drawing on her hypersensitive flesh. Annie bowed off the bed, arching up to him as he suckled strongly, the deep, rhythmic pull sending shockwaves straight to her womb. One hand shaped her other breast, rolling the crest between finger and thumb, driving her crazy. She couldn't halt the sobs the dual assault evoked, her fingers clenching in his hair, holding him to her as she writhed beneath him.

Already she felt as if she was balanced precariously on the precipice of release. 'Nathan, *please*,' she begged, unable to bear the delicious torment.

A gust of warm breath huffed over her painfully aroused areola as he chuckled, subjecting her throbbing nipple to one final long, slow, spine-tingling suck before allowing his prize free. Then his sinful mouth began to trail a zig-zag path of whisper-soft kisses down her abdomen, around her navel, where he lingered for heart-stopping moments, before continuing down her over the gentle curve of her belly. As her thighs parted wantonly to allow him access he settled himself between them. His fingers zeroed in to explore and caress the feminine treasure he discovered, tormenting her with skilful, wicked touches that had her crying out in response.

'I can't stand it,' Annie sobbed, as Nathan traced patterns up the inside of her thigh with the tip of his tongue, getting closer and closer to the very core of her that cried out in desperate need for his attention.

'Yes, you can.' His slow, deliberate, teasing caresses were sensual torture. 'I've waited five years for this— endured five years of misery without you. Now I'm going to take my time and relish every second of doing all the things I've been yearning to do to you for far too long.'

Every part of her was trembling and on fire for him. 'Nathan…'

He stole her breath away with the clever actions of his lips, teeth and tongue as he finally reached her most sensitive flesh. Her hips rose to meet him, but his hands tightened to prevent her moving, holding her where he wanted her, captive to his every desire. Time and again he took her step by step towards the moment of oblivion, only to pull back, refusing to allow her relief. She begged and pleaded until she was hoarse, sure she couldn't survive the intensity of the pleasure. Despite the fact that her heart was racing like a mad thing, her blood felt as thick and sluggish as molasses in her veins. Her hands fisted in the bedsheet as she tried to anchor herself.

Just when she thought she couldn't bear it another second Nathan slid two fingers inside her, immediately finding the hottest spot that threatened to send her straight into orbit, stroking rhythmically, slowly, deeply, and with just the right pressure to make her fear for her sanity.

'It's too much!'

'It's never too much. Come for me, sweetheart. Again.'

He closed his mouth over her clitoris, using his lips and his tongue to send her flying over the edge into the abyss, and the onslaught of ecstasy was too much to cope with as he relentlessly extended and prolonged her climax.

As she gradually floated back to earth, with the aftershocks of her shattering orgasm still undulating through her, Nathan rolled onto his back, taking her with him. He handed her a condom, but she set the foil packet aside, determined to have time to enjoy his body as he had enjoyed hers.

She kissed her way over his chest, lingering to feather

and swirl her tongue around each male nipple in turn, smiling at the way his hands fisted in her hair, at the groan drawn from deep within him. How could she have forgotten the joy of intimately exploring every inch of such masculine perfection? She nibbled her way across his abdomen and then down the narrow line of dark hair to play at his navel, knowing how sensitive he was there, making him toss impatiently beneath her.

Her hands explored, fingers relearning every plane and curve and hollow of his body, finally zeroing in on his impressive erection. He was hot and hard, swelling further to her touch. She loved the feel of him…the softest skin over the steel core. Moving impatiently beneath her, he cursed as she traced his length with her tongue, savouring the musky male taste of him as she took him into her mouth.

Nathan's response was immediate, urging her to hurry. Just as impatient, and unable to wait any longer, she searched for the condom, opened it, and rolled it deftly on before moving to straddle him. His hands skimmed her thighs, stroking over her hips and up her stomach to her breasts. She arched into his touch, her cry mingling with his as she sank down and reunited them with one sure motion.

The feel of him so deep and tight inside her was indescribable. She wanted to stay that way for ever, but he took back control, rolling them again in the tangled sheets until she was beneath him once more. Annie clung to him, wrapping her legs around him, never wanting this to end, scared of what would happen when reality intruded once more. Forcing the thought aside, she lost herself in the fiery magic of loving Nathan—of being loved *by* Nathan—giving everything with her body, heart and soul as fierce pleasure built and built again in an unstoppable swell, overtaking them, sweeping them away on a tidal wave of need and desire.

'Annie…'

As Nathan buried his face in her neck his hold on her tightened, one hand at her nape, his other arm wrapped around her hips. She closed her mouth on his shoulder, tasting the salty heat of his skin. 'Now—please.'

'Yes.'

Crying out in unison, they crested together as her climax triggered his, plunging them into the vortex, racking them with the intensity of release. For a moment Annie thought she actually blacked out. As she slowly regained her senses, gasping for breath, her heart beating a crazy tattoo in her chest, Nathan shifted to one side to ease his weight from her, taking her with him, cradling her against him.

Neither of them spoke. Trying to calm her racing pulse and make sure her lungs were working and receiving oxygen again, Annie nuzzled against him, feeling the frantic beat of his heart beneath her palm. She inhaled the familiar scent of him, mixed with the heat of his body and the musky aroma of their pleasure. It made her feel heady with excitement. She relaxed, spent but exhilarated, soothed by the feel of his fingers stroking her hair, brushing the damp strands back from her flushed face.

Annie wasn't sure what brought her back to herself. Frowning, she realised she must have dozed off. The bedside light had been switched off, and in the dark silence of the bedroom the only sounds were Nathan's steady pulse against her ear and his even breathing. Her head still rested on his chest, but his hold had loosened as he slept. Some of her doubts and anxieties returned as she came more awake and her fogged brain began to clear. What had she done? She needed to think—needed to decide how to explain things to Nathan, was all too aware how much they had to talk about in the cold light of day.

Lifting her head, she was shocked to read the time displayed on the digital clock beside the bed, its figures luminous in the darkness. She'd had no idea it was so late. Due at work early in the morning, she needed to get home. Whilst she hated to leave Nathan, maybe some distance between them would be a good thing. The space would allow them to approach all that had happened—both in the past and tonight—with clearer minds.

Slipping out of bed, already feeling bereft without Nathan's touch, Annie turned on the light in the hallway, using its glow to gather up her discarded clothes. After putting on her boots, she found her jumper on the bedroom floor and pulled it on, unable to bear the restriction of her bra against her sensitised flesh. A blush washed her cheeks when she found her torn panties. Retracing her steps, she discovered her skirt in the living room, and she pulled it on before heading out to the hallway.

'Where are you going?'

About to open the front door, Annie gasped in surprise at the sound of Nathan's sleepily sexy voice behind her and swung round. He looked deliciously rumpled, sated, yet with the spark of hunger still in his eyes. She was relieved he had taken time to pull on his boxer shorts. Faced with the perfection of his body in full naked glory, she wasn't sure she would have survived temptation.

'I'm on early at work, like you. I have to get home,' she explained, wishing she sounded less nervous and awkward. 'Will doesn't know where I am. He'll be worried.'

A tense silence followed, and she saw Nathan's expression close as he shut her off from his thoughts and emotions. Darkly brooding, he closed the distance between them.

'You're going back to him? Now? After what we've just shared?' His anger was evident, and Annie suddenly realised how her words had sounded and the way they had been misconstrued. 'I guess I know where I stand. What was this, Annie? A tumble for old times' sake?'

'No, you don't understand!'

'I understand you're not the woman I thought you were. I'm not a plaything,' he snapped, reaching past her to open the door, allowing in a gust of icy wind.

Annie shivered, more from the hurt disgust and chill in his dark eyes than from the coldness of the weather. 'It's not like that. Please let me explain,' she begged him, distraught at how the situation had run away with her.

'Get out.'

'Nathan—'

His hand closed around her upper arm and she found herself outside before she could explain further. 'I'm not into sharing. I have more respect for myself. And for Will. Even if you don't.'

'Please…'

'We're done, Annie.'

The door closed in her face and the lock snapped shut. She called his name, rang the bell and banged on the door without success. Desperate, she bent down to peer through the letterbox, in time to see Nathan's retreating figure disappear from view. His bedroom door slammed, effectively closing her off from him.

Tears coursed down Annie's cheeks. How could everything have gone so terribly wrong in an instant? How could she have been so *stupid*? Instead of sorting things out she had made them worse—had stumbled and stuttered and given Nathan entirely the wrong impression. The white lie she had told in a moment of desperation that first day he had appeared back in her life had turned into a deception of mammoth proportions. And she had hurt Nathan. Badly. Again. He would never forgive her, even if she tried to explain the web of lies and misunderstandings in which she had entangled them. And why should he? She had done him wrong now, just as she had five years ago.

Nathan thought she had used him and betrayed Will, that she had become the sort of woman who slept around and cheated. She had no one else to blame but herself. This whole situation had rapidly spiralled out of her control. She had tricked Nathan into believing her relationship with Will was a genuine one, so how could she fault him for misunderstanding, for being principled and looking at her with such distaste? She had messed up for a second time in the most awful way possible. Not only hurting him once more but destroying his respect for her and his trust in her. Not to mention any love he still felt for her.

Brushing the tears from her face, she walked unsteadily down the path to her car. Her heart and her soul were shattered. Making love with Nathan again had made her realise how right they were together, how much she had missed him, wanted him in her life. Too late she knew the truth—she loved Nathan with every fibre of her being. She had then and she did now. More than ever. For a second time she had blown it. And thanks to her own stupidity she might never get another chance.

All she could do was go home and try again when she saw him at work the next day, hoping he would have had time to cool down. She had to believe he would listen as she confessed to her mistakes, to her deception. She owed it to him—to them—to lay everything on the line in the hope it wasn't too late. Whether Nathan could ever forgive her was another matter entirely.

* * *

Nathan sat on the bed, numb with shock, battling to re-erect his shattered defences, feeling as if all hope had been stripped from him. The pain was worse than ever, and he was furious with himself for being sucked in again, for allowing himself to believe in fairytales. After their evening making love he had thought there was more than a chance for them, that Annie had come to him wanting to put things right. He'd been a fool a second time.

Her casual remark that she was going home to Will had cut him to the core. Nothing had ever hurt so much. How could she behave that way? *His* Annie would never have done anything like that. And whatever her game-plan was, whatever she thought of him, how could she treat Will so badly? He didn't know this woman at all.

Oppressive loneliness ate away at his insides, doubling him up. He had only himself to blame for his own idiocy, for believing all this time in a love that clearly didn't exist. Not on Annie's side, anyway. She had broken his heart once before and now he'd been stupid enough to let her do it again. Even after five years of pain she had drawn him like a moth to a flame. He'd come here to see her, and had known at once it had been a huge mistake because the love he felt was still there, yet he hadn't been able to make himself leave. She'd remained unfinished business for so long, a wound that refused to heal, and now she had taken a scalpel to that wound and ripped it wide open again.

Cursing aloud, he rose to his feet, switching off the lights as he walked through to the living room. He couldn't stay in the bed—not when it held memories of her, smelled of her. Hell, he'd probably never sleep anyway. He curled up on the sofa in front of the fire, feeling chilled to the bone. Why did he keep torturing himself like this? Why was Annie the one woman he couldn't get out of his head?

It was time for him to face reality, to take off the rose-coloured blinkers. As hard and painful as it was to admit, there could be no future for him with Annie. It was finally over. He couldn't do this any more—would never risk the shattered fragments of his broken heart again. He would have to move on, find somewhere else to start over.

Africa?

There was a job there for him if he wanted it. The prospect didn't fill him with the joy and excitement it should, but he knew it was a place he was needed, somewhere he could make a difference and do something worthwhile. It was also a place where his hurt and loss would count for little compared to the suffering of people he could help. But he knew that even thousands of miles and several countries away Annie would continue to haunt him…

Already feeling on the ragged edge after his latest disaster with Annie the previous night, Nathan choked back emotion as he called the time of death, unable to tear his gaze away from the motionless body of their tiny patient. Tension and despair hung thickly in the atmosphere of the resus bay.

After a sleepless night he had come to work early, both to avoid Annie and to inform his bosses that he would not be staying in Strathlochan. He had arrived at the hospital to find A and E in chaos, with an influx of emergencies co-inciding with the change-over of shifts. Before he could take care of the issue of his resignation he had been called urgently to attend to the collapsed child. Finding that her three-month-old daughter Millie had stopped breathing, Jayne Lewis, who lived two roads away, had rushed the baby in herself rather than wait for an ambulance.

With everyone else assigned to seriously ill patients, Nathan, as the most senior doctor available, had shouldered responsibility, taking Millie to Resus while her distraught mother was comforted in a private room by a nurse. The on-call paediatric consultant had been fast-bleeped, but had been dealing with another emergency on the children's ward and was yet to arrive in A and E. Now it was too late.

After their fruitless attempts to revive little Millie the rest of the staff filed silently away. Whilst they might not show their emotions outwardly, Nathan knew that everyone had been affected by what had happened. One of the nurses stayed behind to clear things away, remove IV lines and disconnect the monitors. Tears clustered on her lashes as she prepared the tiny body, wrapping Millie in a clean, soft blanket so that her mother could hold her one last time. A huge lump lodged in Nathan's throat. He still had to face Jayne Lewis to tell her the news.

Gail, her own eyes moist and filled with sadness, gave him a hug. 'You did everything possible, Nathan. We all did. It's tragic and horrible, but there was really no hope from the moment Millie arrived.'

'If the paediatric consultant had been here—'

'She could have done nothing to change the outcome,' Gail interrupted firmly, staunch in her support and understanding.

Nathan nodded, holding on to his composure by a thread. In his head he knew Gail was right, but it didn't take away the pain and helplessness of the last thirty minutes. Although showing no signs of rigidity or blood pooling, they had all known there was zero chance of saving Millie. Yet she had been intubated at once, chest compressions started. Unable to find any viable vein, Nathan had inserted a needle into a leg bone in order to rapidly deliver fluids and drugs. Nothing had worked. There had been no hope. But they had had to try—for Millie, for her mother, for themselves.

'I'll come with you to see the mother.'

'Thanks, Gail.' Unable to produce a smile, he rested a hand on her shoulder, grateful for her empathy. 'You don't have to.'

'Yes, I do. We're in it together with this job. The good and the bad.'

Following the standard procedure in place in this hospital, Nathan went to the room where Jayne Lewis waited with the nurse assigned to comfort her. Jayne's aunt and a friend had arrived, to add their support. Breaking bad news was something that never became easier, Nathan thought, but he sat beside the shocked, sobbing woman, holding her hand as he tried to explain the unexplainable. Millie—healthy, happy and well-loved—had been a victim of sudden infant death syndrome.

The awful task completed, Gail accompanied Jayne to see Millie while he shut himself in the office and forced himself to focus on completing the official paperwork. He had to inform the Procurator Fiscal of the death, as well as ensure that all samples and notes were properly labelled and recorded before he signed off on them. Next he arranged for photographs, should Jayne want them, then organised a bereavement counsellor and notified the GP, so that follow-up care would be offered.

Nothing changed the outcome.

Millie had died.

It was the worst start possible to a dreadful day, and he didn't even want to think what else could go wrong.

Desperate for some space and a cup of tea, Nathan left the office and headed to the staffroom—only to run into Annie. He couldn't deal with her now. Just looking at her hurt. Thankful that there were other people in the room, he kept his back to Annie and switched on the kettle, wishing he didn't still want her despite everything. Why was he such a fool over this woman? He knew he had to walk away to save his own sanity, so why was it so hard to do?

CHAPTER EIGHT

NATHAN looked dreadful.

Constrained by the presence of the others in the room, Annie bit her lip and watched in silence as he stood at the worktop and made a cup of tea. His back was ramrod-straight, his shoulders stiff—everything about his pose screamed unapproachability.

She hadn't slept a wink last night. And she had arrived home, tearful and in despair, only to find that Will wasn't even there. He had been out with Anthony. Her flight from Nathan's, her thoughtless words that had hurt him so deeply and created completely the wrong impression, had all been for nothing. Feeling horribly alone, she had curled up on her bed, her arms wrapped around herself, her brain struggling to come up with a workable plan on how to explain things to Nathan.

Her gaze lingered on his tense, silent frame. Even the shapeless scrubs he wore couldn't detract from his impressive looks and masculinity. At the moment he refused to even look at her, so how was she ever going to get him to listen to what she needed to say? It would be difficult, but she had to tell him the whole truth…and then she could only hope he could forgive her.

She couldn't imagine the rest of her life without Nathan being part of it. Or how she had survived the last five years without him. The extent of her self-delusion, her denial and her mistakes took her breath away. As did the uncomfortable knowledge that she had never even considered how Nathan might have felt when she had left him. She'd been so selfish. Where had he been these last five years? What had happened to him? And why wasn't he a specialist registrar already?

She had so many questions but, having kept him at arm's length and lied to him, the tables were now turned on her and it was Nathan who was blanking *her*.

Annie's troubled thoughts were interrupted when the staffroom door opened and Will all but bounced into the room. In contrast to Nathan's pale face and bleak expression, Will looked happiness personified—a fact that didn't go unnoticed by the other staff in the room.

'You look even more disgustingly chipper than normal, Will,' one of the nurses teased him. 'I thought you were off today?'

'I swapped shifts with Gus—Julia isn't feeling well, so he's taking her for a check-up with her obstetrician.'

As Will explained his unexpected presence, Annie noticed Nathan heading towards the door. She rose to her feet, determined to follow him and try to arrange a time to talk. Before she could move, however, Will was scooping her up and swinging her around.

'And I *am* disgustingly chipper,' he said, laughing in answer to the other part of the nurse's comment. 'Because I'm in love!'

Seeing the hurt and anger in Nathan's dark eyes as he cast her one fulminating glare before leaving the room, Annie smothered a cry of frustration and wriggled out of Will's arms.

'What's wrong?' he asked, stepping back, a frown of concern sobering his face.

'I'll explain later,' she whispered, anxious that no one should overhear. 'I have to catch Nathan.'

By the time she reached the corridor Nathan was striding ahead of her and about to disappear around the corner. She ran after him, calling his name. He hesitated, glancing over his shoulder, clearly reluctant to stop.

'Please,' she begged as she closed the distance between them, conscious that other people were milling about, affording them no privacy.

'Not now, Annie.'

'When, then?' An edge of desperation crept into her voice. 'I need to talk to you—to explain things.'

He strode off towards the A and E department. 'I'm not interested in whatever arrangement you have going on with Will.'

'It's not like that!'

She wanted to protest further, but was worried about making a scene in public. The department was hectic, crowded with staff and patients, and already people were looking at them. However much she wanted this settled, she couldn't shout out in front of everyone that Will was gay. Neither did she want her colleagues to know how badly she had behaved, nor that she had lied. Caught in a trap of her own making, she could do nothing but wait.

As Nathan walked away from her Annie hesitated, unsure whether to go after him or not. Wrestling with indecision, she was startled when Gail came up beside her.

'Give him some space, love,' the older nurse advised.

'Sorry?'

Gail's smile was understanding. 'Now isn't the best

time for Nathan,' she added, explaining what had happened with baby Millie.

'Oh, no.' A lump lodged in Annie's throat. She wanted to go to him, to comfort him, but she feared his rejection. 'Nathan will be devastated.'

'He's taking it hard. It was upsetting for all the team.'

'No matter how many times you see these things, you never get hardened to it,' Annie mused sadly.

'You and Nathan are such good doctors because you haven't lost your compassion and the ability to care.' Gail gave her hand a squeeze. 'I've sensed from the first that you two have something of a history. It's the way you look at each other. Whatever's gone wrong, Annie, I'm sure you can work things out.'

Touched, Annie managed a watery smile. 'Thanks, Gail.'

As the kindly woman left, Annie sucked in a ragged breath. She hoped her friend was right and it wasn't already too late to make amends with Nathan. From across the crowded department she saw him standing at the desk, reviewing the next set of case notes from the tray. He looked so distant, so sad, so alone. And it was all her fault.

There was nothing she could do at this moment to right the wrongs she had committed against him, but later she would try again. Despite all the setbacks, she was determined she was going to see this through. Far too late she acknowledged just how much she had always loved him—still loved him. Whether or not she had hurt him one too many times for him to forgive her, and whether or not they could ever have another chance at being together, she wouldn't rest until she had apologised and explained everything—she owed Nathan that much at least.

* * *

With the department stretched to capacity, Annie scarcely had a moment to draw breath. Amongst the many patients she saw, whose problems were varied and ranged in levels of seriousness, were two regulars. One was a nineteen-year-old girl battling a drug problem, who had been brought in for the second time since Christmas after being assaulted by a man who had picked her up on a street corner. Annie was very concerned at the danger the girl was placing herself in as she tried to get money to feed her habit. Frustrated that the system and target pressures didn't allow her the time necessary to spend talking to the girl, Annie finally persuaded her to visit the drop-in clinic, where she would get full support, care and advice from Thorn and his staff and hopefully help to come off the drugs and get her life back on track.

Her second regular was a middle-aged alcoholic man who had been found collapsed in one of the town's parks by a morning dog-walker. He had apparently fallen while making his unsteady way home from the pub in the early hours, spending the night in the cold with a broken leg that needed plating, a very sore head and mild hypothermia. Annie finished the paperwork and handed him—and the battle with the hospital's bed manager for an admission slot—over to the orthopaedic registrar.

Although time passed in a blur of activity, she found it uncharacteristically hard to focus on her job. All she could think about was Nathan. She caught herself straining to hear the sound of his voice, or trying to catch a glimpse of him as she hurried from Reception to waiting room to examination cubicle, from one patient to another.

A couple of hours ago, while chasing up X-ray and blood test results for a twenty-seven-year old man with sudden-onset abdominal pain and vomiting, who had been given analgesia and was being monitored pending further investigations, she had managed to exchange a few words with Will—sufficient to inform him of her latest *faux pas* with Nathan.

'For someone who is normally so intelligent, sensible and attuned to people's feelings, you've been a complete idiot over Nathan,' he'd told her, shaking his head and holding nothing back. 'You have to tell him everything, Annie.'

'I'm trying to! But he won't speak to me. Not that I blame him.'

Thankfully Will had refrained from saying *I told you so*.

Back in A and E, and with the results of the young man's tests suggesting caecal volvulus—a twisting of the bowel—she signed him over to the surgical team, who were anticipating the need to perform a right hemicolectomy to correct the problem. Next she was caught up in treating casualties of the third motorway traffic collision of the day. She had long since given up hope of grabbing a reviving cup of coffee, let alone any lunch.

She was at the desk, wiping the details of the patient she had just dealt with off the whiteboard, when further chaos erupted in the shape of two burly, heavily tattooed men. Dripping blood from assorted cuts and bruises, they were escorted inside by five harrassed-looking police officers. Voices were raised and language was foul. The entourage had barely crossed the threshold before the head receptionist, without whom the department would cease to function, was calling for additional security and organising things so that existing patients would be disturbed as little as possible by the new arrivals.

Robert Mowbray emerged from an examination cubicle to speak to the police sergeant in charge, and Annie hovered at Reception in case she was needed, instinctively keeping herself between the children's play area nearby—where a volunteer nurse was keeping watch over three youngsters—and the swearing, bloodied men, who were trying to fight each other *and* the policemen struggling to restrain them.

As the scuffle intensified, one of the arrested men made a bid for freedom, punching one of his captors and knocking aside the other. With the A and E exit guarded, the man turned, his eyes wild and frantic as he searched for another means of escape. To reach the corridor to the rest of the hospital he'd have to go by the children, Annie realised, and with no other thought in her mind than sheltering them she maintained her position.

The panicked man closed the gap between them. Annie heard shouts before the man grabbed her. Then she was aware of a sharp bloom of pain in her chest, and she glanced down in disbelief to see the man withdraw what looked like a screwdriver clutched in his hand.

Shocked, Annie cried out as he shoved her roughly aside. Disorientated, she felt herself falling. Unable to slow the momentum, she hit the floor with a thud. She thought she heard Nathan's familiar voice calling her name, and she tried unsuccessfully to lift her head to look for him, but her vision was blurry. People were yelling. An alarm was sounding. Running footsteps pounded closer. She knew a warm wetness on her skin under the top of her scrubs. Once again she tried to open her eyes, but they wouldn't obey. She felt strange. Scared. Nathan's name was a whisper on her lips. She had the crazy thought that he would never know she loved him. Then everything went black.

Having spent time stitching up a deep cut on the leg of a middle-aged woman brought to A and E by her sister,

Nathan had just finished referring her to Dr Cameron Kincaid, a specialist in self-harm at the Ackerman Centre, on the outskirts of town, when he had heard the commotion in Reception. Advising the two women to wait in the cubicle, he had stepped out from behind the curtain to see what was happening, his horrified gaze taking in the scene unfolding before him as if it was happening in slow motion.

An injured man had broken away from the police officers attempting to restrain him, and his attempt to flee was taking him close to Annie, who was near the play area. Before Nathan could react, the man was grabbing Annie, shouting obscenities. Then his arm rose, and Nathan saw that he had something clutched in his hand. It looked like a screwdriver, and he wondered how the man had managed to secrete it and get it past the policemen. He watched in horror as the man plunged his hand down at Annie's chest, before pushing her away and rushing towards the opening to the corridor out of the department.

'Annie!'

Nathan rushed towards her, but he was too late to catch her before she hit the floor. The next moment he was kneeling beside her, every part of him shaking in fear as he looked at her too-pale face, her closed eyes. She was unconscious, failing to respond to him, her pulse thready. He checked her head and could find no sign of a fracture or a cut, although a bump was forming. And then he saw the welling of blood beginning to stain the top of her baggy scrubs.

'Oh, God. No.' Whilst aware of activity all around him, as the police and hospital security attempted to apprehend the fleeing assailant and control his cohort, Nathan's sole focus was on the woman he loved. 'Resus!' he shouted, drawing attention to the desperateness of the situation. 'I need help here. Annie's been stabbed.'

There was little time to lose, and Nathan scooped Annie up in his arms and carried her swiftly but gently to the resus bay, setting her down on a trolley bed just as Gail rushed to his side, immediately beginning to help him attach monitors and check Annie's vital signs.

'Her blood pressure is low and falling,' Nathan announced, his voice rough with emotion he couldn't hide. 'Come on, sweetheart. Hold on,' he pleaded with her as he worked. 'Stay with me, Annie.'

Two more nurses and a junior doctor arrived, wasting no time asking questions but setting to work doing what was needed, including cutting off Annie's scrubs to reveal the site of a penetrating stab wound by her left breast, immediately over her heart. The doctor in him knew this had to be done. The man in him wanted to cover Annie up, to protect her from indignities and exposure.

He swiftly studied the chest wound. The hole looked small, but Nathan knew from experience that the damage inside could be deadly. They needed to know what was going on and get the bleeding stopped as soon as possible. He'd always been calm, whatever the crisis, but this was his Annie, and his hands were uncharacteristically shaky as he tried to find a vein and insert a cannula in her arm.

'Nathan, step aside,' Will instructed, taking the needle from him.

'Will—'

'You're too close, mate. Trust me.' The other man was firm, in control, focused on inserting the cannula with the minimum of fuss. 'Robert's on his way. So is the anaesthetist. And Francesca—we'll need an ultrasound scan of Annie's chest.'

Thankfully, both Francesca and the anaesthetist were still in the department after the day's various emergencies, and were there in seconds.

'Equal bilateral air entry—even breath sounds. No indication of pneumothorax,' the anaesthetist reported. 'Oxygen saturation ninety per cent, respiration rate twenty. How's her heart?'

'BP's still dropping and cardiac output is unstable. Pulse thready,' Gail informed him.

The anaesthetist worked swiftly, choosing drugs and muscle relaxant with care. He soon had an endotracheal tube inserted, and Annie fully anaesthetised and ventilated.

Nathan had to move away briefly as Francesca took a chest X-ray, but he returned at once to Annie's right side, clutching her hand, feeling helpless and more frightened than he had ever been. He stared in numb disbelief, unable to move, his brain fuzzed as all his knowledge deserted him at the shock and pain of seeing Annie's life draining away in front of him. He shook his head, trying to pull himself together.

'I'm thinking cardiac tamponade,' he said, as Robert Mowbray stepped up on Annie's other side.

'Get a chest drain in, Will, and gain central venous access,' the consultant demanded as he carried out a thorough examination and double checked the vital signs. 'Fast-bleep the cardiothoracic consultant. Are the fluids warm? I want blood cross-matched.'

'Annie is A positive,' Nathan told him.

'Are you sure?'

'One hundred per cent certain. We went as blood donors together for several years.'

Robert barked out an order for six units of A positive blood and a nurse scurried to the phone. 'How's the BP?'

'It's still dropping,' Gail replied, worry evident on her face. 'Eighty over forty now.'

'Annie hit her head on the floor when she fell,' Nathan

remembered, furious he had not passed on that information sooner.

'We'll worry about a CT scan when we have her stabilised,' Robert replied, turning to the radiographer as she did a follow-up ultrasound. 'Francesca, what news?'

'Definite fluid in the pericardium,' Francesca confirmed, moving back out of the way and showing Robert the images from the X-ray and scan.

Nathan's panic intensified. Why didn't they *hurry*? He wanted to push them all aside and do the job himself, but he recognised that he was too emotional, too unsteady to be safe. He could see from the monitors that Annie was failing. Something bad was going on inside her chest, and the team needed to work fast if they were to save her life. His fingers linked with hers as he tried to instil her with the strength and determination to keep fighting, even though she was unconscious and couldn't hear him.

'Damn, the blood is pouring out of this drain,' Will called, sounding shaken.

'We're losing her,' Robert muttered.

'No! She's *not* going to die.' Nathan refused to countenance such an outcome. Whatever had happened last night, or for the last five years, he couldn't lose her. He *couldn't*. 'I won't let her.'

'There's no time to get to Theatre. We'll have to do a thoracotomy here. Now. Before it's too late.'

The consultant's decision brought Nathan a mix of relief and terror. Relief that someone was going to do something—the only thing that could now save Annie's life—and terror that it wouldn't work. An emergency thoracotomy, which involved opening up the chest to expose her heart, was high risk—especially outside the operating room. But without it Annie would die. Nathan had assisted in a few, and had done one once during his surgical rotation years before, but only under proper theatre conditions. He wondered at the A and E consultant's experience with the procedure.

As if sensing his troubled thoughts, Will took a moment to reassure him. 'Robert's done this successfully several times,' he murmured, as the thoracotomy tray was readied.

Nathan was absorbing what Will had said when Gail called out more bad news. 'BP's fallen.'

'Central venous pressure?' Robert asked, frowning at the reply.

A nurse wiped Annie's chest with generous quantities of a povidone-iodine antiseptic solution, to disinfect and prepare her pale skin for the operation, then Annie's left arm was raised above her head to give access to the site. Feeling helpless, Nathan watched as Robert skilfully opened the chest wall at the medial end of the fifth intercostal space and made a lateral cut above the sixth rib into the axilla. Retractors opened the cavity. Needing more space to work and access the heart, Robert extended the incision and separated the sternum. It seemed as if everyone in the resus bay held their collective breath as the consultant worked as swiftly as possible, making a longitudinal incision in the pericardium—the blue-coloured sac surrounding the heart, which had been punctured by the screwdriver. There was so much blood...

'Suction!' Robert called, and a nurse hurried to comply, keeping the cavity clear so he could see what he was doing.

Nathan wanted to remind the consultant to take extra care not to damage the phrenic nerve, but he managed to halt the words as he saw Robert move to increase the pericardial incision with his fingers to avoid lacerating the nerve. He was no doubt already annoying everyone by demanding updates on Annie's vital signs, Nathan acknowledged, but they were kind enough to humour him, and he was grateful for their tolerance and that he'd not been banished from the room.

'There's a hole in the right ventricle,' Robert announced, once the heart itself was exposed.

Will's voice cut across the electric silence. 'She's arrested!'

'Nathan, put your finger in the hole,' the consultant ordered, maintaining his composure. 'And do bimanual internal massage.'

He didn't think, he just acted, plugging the wound and stopping the haemorrhage, using the flat of both hands on either side of the heart to maintain a rhythmic compression. Having something constructive to do kept him focused. Despite having done this once before, he felt a moment of awe and wonder that he actually held *Annie's* heart in his hands. The responsibility was overwhelming.

Aware of Will beside him, it occurred to him for the first time to question why the other man was working as normal on Annie while he himself had been told to stand aside because he was too involved. Surely the same applied to Will? He shook his head, too stressed to fret about it now. He just wanted Annie safe. So did the team. They all cared about Annie and would give everything for her now.

'The A positive blood is here,' a nurse called, hurrying into the room.

'Good.' Robert didn't look up from his task, suctioning the remaining clots and blood from the cavity around the heart and checking for any other sites of damage. 'Will, get the first unit up and running in.'

When the consultant was ready to begin suturing the wound in the chamber of the heart Nathan had to adjust his hands to give him room to work. His own heart was in his mouth as Robert closed the hole in Annie's right ventricle, using uninterrupted non-absorbable proline sutures buttressed with teflon pledgets. It seemed to be taking for ever, but he knew it was only minutes before the task was done and her bleeding stopped.

'Cardiac rhythm and output?' Robert requested.

Gail was ready with the information. 'She's fibrillating.'

'Internal paddles.'

They were immediately placed in Robert's hands, and as Nathan withdrew he inserted them into Annie's chest, one over each side of her heart, ready to deliver the electric shock to defibrillate and bring back a rhythm.

'Five joules to start.'

'Still fibrillating,' Gail called, after the first jolt had been given.

'Again … ten joules this time.'

Nathan stared at the tracing on the monitor and prayed as he'd never prayed before. It took three more attempts, with increasing amounts of energy, before Annie's heart began to beat on its own.

'We have a pulse!' The announcement from Gail brought a cheer to the room. 'And a rhythm!'

'OK, let's guard against hypovolaemia and any cardiac concussion,' Robert directed.

'Cardiac output is stabilising,' Will updated, giving details of the central venous pressure, too. 'And her BP's up; her pulse is strong.'

'Sats are improving. We're up to ninety five per cent and rising,' the anaesthetist added, a broad smile on his face.

Nathan wanted to burst with joyful relief. They still had a way to go, a voice in his head cautioned, but Annie was back and clinging to life, and he wasn't going to allow her to do anything less. Still tense, he watched closely as Robert closed the pericardium with vertical mattress sutures. Will and Gail continued to gave updates on Annie's stabilising cardiac output and rising BP.

'I can't see any damage to the lungs, major vessels or anything else,' Robert commented in apparent satisfaction, doing a thorough examination now the bleeding had been stopped. Nathan's relief increased. 'Insert an arterial line and a urinary catheter,' he instructed. 'And redo U&E, glucose, FBC and clotting. I'll ligate the internal mammary arteries and then we'll defer to the cardiothoracic surgeon for further management. He can double-check everything and do the closure in Theatre.' Robert glanced up and looked at him. 'I assume you'll be going up with Annie?'

'Yes, please.' Nathan was grateful for the understanding. 'Thank you—for saving her.' He looked round the bay at all the colleagues who had worked so swiftly and diligently, trying to keep his wayward emotions in check. 'Thank you all.'

Nodding, allowing a brief smile of his own, Robert concentrated once more on what he was doing and called for antibiotics. 'Give cefuroxime 1.5g IV.'

The next minutes passed in a blur as the specialist, Gordon Smith, arrived, with a couple of his assistants, and was brought up to date on the details. He was handed a copy of the notes, with information on all drugs, fluids and bloods given. He cast a curious glance at Nathan, who clung determinedly to Annie's hand as she was prepared for the transfer.

'Good job,' Gordon said, in praise of Robert's handiwork.

Then they were whisking the trolley away from Resus, through the still crowded but calmer A and E department, and up to the operating theatre, where the rest of the cardiothoracic team were ready to go.

Nathan was upset when the surgeon refused him entry to the theatre, but he didn't waste time arguing, knowing that it was Annie who was important here, not his own feelings. He sank to a chair in the waiting area, nervous exhaustion overwhelming him. Shaking, he put his head in his hands, hardly able to take in everything that had happened in the last half an hour, or how close Annie had come to dying. His scrubs were covered in her blood. So were his hands. As he became aware that the other people in the room were looking at him nervously, he rose to his feet and walked stiffly and unsteadily to the nearest restroom to clean up.

That done, he stopped at the office on his way back to use the phone and ring Annie's mother. It was one of the most difficult calls he'd ever had to make. Eve was understandably shocked and emotional. Nathan reassured her as best he could, only hanging up when she sounded more together, knowing she would make arrangements to travel to Strathlochan straight away.

Bone weary, he went back to the waiting room. To keep himself focused and hang on to the threads of his control, he closed his eyes and imagined what was happening in the operating theatre. In his head he went through the details of how the surgeon would be ensuring there was no other internal damage before methodically rejoining the sternum using wire, then suturing closed the muscle, tissue and skin of Annie's chest.

Footsteps sounded in the corridor and Nathan looked up, hope and tension warring inside him as he anticipated that Annie's operation was over. But it was Will who appeared in the waiting area, and slumped into a seat beside him with a heavy sigh.

'Any news yet?'

Nathan shook his head. 'No.'

'Someone should call Annie's mother,' Will suggested.

'I've already done it. Eve's on her way.'

Will gave his shoulder a quick pat. 'Thanks, mate.'

Time dragged. Each tick of the second hand on the clock on the wall dragged. Nathan was scarcely aware of the other people in the room, who were also stressed and worried and waiting for news of their loved ones. Will disappeared for a few moments, returning with two mugs of tea, but Nathan barely tasted the hot brew.

'She'll be OK, Nathan. Annie's tough…a fighter.'

They looked at each other in silent acknowledgement, united in anxiety and pain.

'Yeah.' He wanted to believe it. He *had* to believe it.

'We should talk.'

Will's words filled Nathan with a whole new kind of concern. But whatever the other man was about to say was forestalled as Gordon Smith appeared in the doorway, dressed in his scrubs, his protective cap still on his head and his face mask hanging loosely now around his neck.

'Later,' Nathan commented in response to Will, rising to his feet and crossing to greet the cardiothoracic consultant. 'What's the news on Annie?'

'She's going to be fine,' the surgeon reassured them.

'Thank God.'

Nathan seconded Will's exclamation. 'And thank you, Mr Smith. Can you update us on Annie's condition?'

'Of course.' The surgeon led them to an office across the hall and gestured for them to sit as he walked around the desk to take his own chair. 'We found no further internal damage. Robert did an excellent emergency repair. After the operation to close was over we sent her for a CT scan, and I'm happy to say that there is no sign of any skull

fracture and no clots or bleeding on the brain,' he continued. Nathan felt another welling of relief and gratitude. 'At
the moment she is heavily sedated and being moved to the
Intensive Care Unit. When she does wake up she's going
to have a hell of a headache, not to mention discomfort
from the surgery. We'll keep her medicated, of course, and
watch for any signs of complications, but all being well she
should make a good recovery.'

Nathan slumped back on the chair with a sigh, some of
the tension leaching from him. He knew Annie was likely
to be in hospital for between five to ten days, providing
there were no setbacks, and that she would then need time
to recuperate. But she was alive. Whatever they faced in
the days and weeks ahead—and whatever role he played—
that was the fact that he had to hang on to.

'Can we see her?' Will asked.

The surgeon looked from one to the other, clearly puzzled
at the dynamics of this relationship. 'Briefly—for now.'

Conscious of Will keeping pace beside him, Nathan
made his way to the ICU. He guessed that Gordon Smith
had phoned ahead, because the charge nurse was there to
greet them and take them to Annie's bedside.

Will's indrawn hiss of breath matched his own. The
sight of Annie so still and pale, looking swamped and
fragile in the bed, hooked up to machines and drips and
drains, brought a fresh constriction to Nathan's throat. No
matter that they were doctors and saw this every day. It was
different when it was personal to you.

Drawn at once to Annie's side, Nathan took her hand,
holding fingers that felt cool and lifeless against his cheek.
He would give anything not to have rowed with her, for last
night's lovemaking to have ended with them being back
together and not further apart than ever. But more than

anything, whatever happened between them, he just needed
for her to live, to heal, to be well.

He started when Will rested a hand on his shoulder.
'Sorry,' he mumbled, feeling a mix of guilt and resentment
as he stepped back to give the other man access to Annie,
hating that Will had more right to be with her than he did.

'I'll cover for you in A and E,' Will announced, after
staring down at Annie for several moments in silence, an
almost greyish tinge to his normally healthy complexion.
'You stay with her. We'll have that talk later.'

Without another word, Will hurried from the ward.
Nathan couldn't understand Will at all, but, no matter how
puzzled he was at his exit, at his whole reaction to Annie's
trauma, he was grateful to be the one remaining by her side.
Pulling up a chair, he sat down, taking Annie's hand back
in his. Listening to the rhythmic sounds of the machines,
and instinctively monitoring her vital signs, he stayed as
close to her as he was able, talking to her, giving her his
strength, his love, everything he had within him, so that she
would pull through.

He wasn't leaving until he knew she was safe.

And so began his vigil.

CHAPTER NINE

'ANNIE, open your eyes.'

The voice seemed to come from a long way off, fighting its way through the layers of pain gripping her body and the fog of confusion muddling her brain. Annie had heard the voice calling to her before. Nathan's voice. Warm and husky, concerned and cajoling.

'Come on, sweetheart, you can do it. Look at me.'

She frowned as the command sounded louder and more focused, urging her to obey. Struggling through the darkness, she tried to remember where she was, what had happened, but she couldn't seem to catch hold of anything tangible. Her thoughts were random, scattered, hazy. Time had no meaning. But for long minutes, or maybe it was hours, she listened to that voice. Several times she thought she heard her mother calling her, too, but Annie felt too lethargic and too far away from them to reach out.

If she tried to move her whole body screamed in protest. She groaned. Or thought she did. But her throat felt so raw she wasn't sure any sound emerged. It felt as if an elephant was sitting on top of her—an elephant that had first skewered her chest with a red-hot sabre and smacked her on the back of the head with a tree trunk.

'Can you hear me, Annie?' Fingertips feathered across her forehead and down her cheek. She was aware of the sensation, and tried to turn her face towards the touch. 'That's it, sweetheart. Come back to us. Can you squeeze my hand, Annie?'

She felt the warmth and strength of Nathan's hand holding hers. It took almost more effort and concentration than she could muster, but she compelled her fingers to close over his.

'Good girl!'

She basked in the praise, then felt her hand being lifted before lips and warm breath brushed across her skin. Drawing on her flagging reserves, she tried to prise stubborn eyelids apart. For a moment Nathan's face swam muzzily into view. He looked drawn and tired, a shadow of stubble darkening his jaw. Somewhere inside her she knew that he shouldn't be here with her, but she was very glad he was. Lips that felt dry and unwieldy parted, but his name sounded more like a hoarse, whispery moan than anything else.

Overwhelmingly tired, she allowed her eyes to close again. Her head was throbbing, and moving it made her feel nauseous. She was aware of other voices in the background but she tuned out the words, focusing on Nathan's nearness, on the reality of his fingers linked with hers. Then she felt the brush of something cool…an ice cube on her parched lips. She parted them, welcoming the blissfully chilled melting water drizzling over them and into the rawness of her mouth and throat.

Why did she hurt so much? Why couldn't she move? As she grappled with the disorientation a single tear welled from the corner of one eye. She felt it escape and track down her face, and then the pad of Nathan's thumb was there to catch it, gently soothing across her cheek before his hand moved to stroke her hair.

'You're going to be fine, Annie.'

Nathan's words and his calm, compelling voice reassured her, and she clung to him with all her will, as if he was a lifebuoy keeping her safe and protected, holding her head above water in a stormy, turbulent sea.

'I'm sure you're confused and hurting and feeling scared, but everything will be all right. Your mum's here, sweetheart, and so is Will, and your friends…and me.'

The last sounded hesitant, unsure, but she was too weak to question or protest. The gentle massage of his fingers relaxed her and she felt herself slipping away again.

'We're looking after you. Try not to worry about anything. Sleep now, and get well.'

Wondering what it was she had to get well from, and why all those people were coming to see her, Annie sighed and allowed the darkness to reclaim her.

Nathan had lost track of time. The first hours had passed in a blur of anxiety as he maintained his vigil at Annie's bedside, refusing to leave her until he knew that she was out of danger.

Eve had arrived, worried sick about her daughter, and he had done his best to hide his own fears and reassure her. She had moved in to the spare room at his rented flat close to the hospital for the duration of her stay, but, like him, most of her time was spent at Annie's side.

It had been a huge relief for everyone when Annie had begun to come round, and those first moments when she had opened her eyes, squeezed his hand and tried to say his name were impinged on his memory. He had been so full of joy and gratitude, and so emotionally and physically exhausted after the endless hours of living with fear and without sleep, that he had needed to shut himself in the men's room to compose himself.

Annie had made good progress since then. Although she continued to sleep for long periods, she gradually became more awake and aware, and she had left the ICU after two days and been moved to a quiet room on the surgical ward. Which was when another problem had reared its head. Annie had no recollection of the assault, or the hours leading up to it. A second precautionary CT scan had been done, but Annie had been given the all-clear. There was no swelling of the brain, no bleeding, no clot, no hidden fracture…nothing physical to cause concern.

'Post-concussion syndrome and post-traumatic amnesia,' the doctor sent to assess Annie had diagnosed. 'It's not uncommon, but no one can say how quickly she'll remember the missing hours.'

The last thing she remembered was driving down to visit her mother. Which meant she had no recollection of making love with him, or of the difficult situation between them afterwards when she had left his bed to return to Will. Hurt pierced him even now. Although he knew that it was unlikely to have changed what had happened in A and E later, he felt guilty for not listening to her when she had wanted to talk to him. Now, though, as Annie asked more questions and became more alert, her lack of memory made things awkward, and Eve, Will and himself were trying to be careful what they said.

The police had come to take statements. Nathan had given his, as had the other staff who had been present in A and E when Annie had been stabbed, but it would be a while before Annie was well enough to speak to them…*if* she regained her memories of the incident. Thankfully the man who had assaulted her had been caught and charged and was now in custody.

Many of Annie's friends and colleagues had been to visit and encourage her recovery, and her hospital room was awash with flowers and fruit and chocolates. Aside from Eve, Will and himself, the most regular visitors were Gail from A and E, Holly Tait, who popped down from the children's ward during her breaks, and Francesca, who came in from the radiology department and spent some time sitting with Annie before leaving for home so that whoever was with her could have a break and get something to eat. Gina and Seb had visited several times, as had Callie and Frazer, all worried about their friend. And Nathan had met self-harm specialist Cameron Kincaid for the first time, when he had called in with his wife and partner in the Ackerman Clinic, Dr Ginger O'Neill, who ran the eating disorders unit.

Nathan was grateful for their kindness and concern, as well as being both touched and puzzled by their support of him. Everyone had rallied round, and his colleagues in the A and E department were making it as easy as possible for him to take time off to be at Annie's bedside. Chief amongst those smoothing things over and covering his workload was Will. Which Nathan still couldn't understand. Surely Will and not him had the right to priority treatment where Annie was concerned? But even Eve deferred to Nathan, seeking his advice about any medical decisions and placing him as important in Annie's life, although she was also clearly friendly with Will.

As Annie regained her strength, and started to spend spells each day sitting in a chair and taking short walks aided by the physiotherapy team, Nathan knew the time was coming when reality had to be faced and decisions made.

Any day now she would be discharged to convalesce at home, and what would happen then? Would Will take over once more, relegating him to the margins and excluding him from Annie's life? Would Annie remember their lovemaking and what had happened between them? The more alert she became, the more nervous and guarded she appeared around him. Any moment now she could choose Will, and Nathan would find himself out in the cold once more.

'I'm so confused about everything.'

Sitting in an armchair beside the bed in her hospital room, Annie sighed, grimacing as even that small action tightened her chest with pain. Her head felt much better now, the concussion having abated and with it the feelings of nausea and dizziness, but even with the medication she was on the rest of her remained uncomfortable.

'Are you remembering more now?' her mother asked, a guarded expression on her face as she glanced up from her task of peeling and coring an apple.

'Some things,' Annie admitted, equally cautious, because the snippets of things she *did* recall made her ashamed and embarrassed and very scared. 'I still don't have any memories of what happened in A and E.'

The worry that had been etched on her mother's face for days was still apparent as she frowned. 'Maybe that's a good thing?' she suggested, handing over some slices of apple.

'Maybe.'

Annie plucked a piece of fruit from the plate and nibbled at it, lost in her thoughts. The overriding concern that plagued her was Nathan. Fragments had come back to her over the last few days. Enough that she could piece events together and remember how terribly she had behaved—not only five years ago but more recently. Lying to him, making love to him, and letting him believe she was involved with another man. Despite everything she had done to him Nathan had saved her life, had selflessly been by her side the entire time, urging her to live, to get well, helping her mother, generally making everything more bearable, driving himself to the point of exhaustion.

She would never forget listening to his voice, or the way he had made her feel safe and grounded, her light in the darkness. As she had dozed and drifted during those first couple of days he had talked softly to her of the happy times they had shared in the past, relaxing her, soothing her, reminding her of funny incidents from medical school, warming her with tender memories of their life together. She would never forget the other things he had said to her, too—things that were slowly making sense...

'I love you, Annie...so much,' he had whispered, while she had still been disorientated and in ICU. His words had been heartfelt and sincere, so soft she'd barely heard them. 'I'm sorry I didn't listen when you tried to talk to me. If you want Will and not me I'll go away and never bother you again. Just get better, sweetheart.'

Now, when she was nearly ready to go home, she sensed Nathan putting more distance between them—pulling back from her physically and emotionally, as if he believed he wasn't welcome or wanted. He did more hours in A and E— which meant less time spent with her. What terrified her was that once she left the hospital Nathan would leave her and Strathlochan. There had been no opportunity to talk, with so many other people coming and going, and only in the last day or so had she sorted through all her scattered memories and faced the truth. A truth she still hadn't told him.

Annie closed her eyes as tears stung them. She couldn't seem to stop crying just lately, but she knew much of that was reaction to all she had been through. Whilst she might not remember all that had happened, she had been told the details. She knew she had been stabbed, knew she would have died if not for Nathan's quick thinking in getting her to Resus and starting to treat her before Robert Mowbray had taken over to do the thoracotomy.

'Are you all right, love?'

She swallowed down the foolish tears and opened her eyes, trying to smile for her mother without success, unable to force any words past the restriction in her throat.

'Oh, Annie.' Her mother inched closer and took her hand. 'I wish I could stay longer—or take you home with me.'

'We've discussed this. Your job is important. You have to go back. I'm just grateful you've been here through the worst of it.'

'I know, but—'

Annie gently forestalled her protests. 'Really, it's all right. And as for when I leave here, I just want to be in my own place. I have loads of people who will help me. There's Will, of course, and…' Her words trailed off, and she battled down a fresh welling of emotion as her thoughts turned once more to Nathan.

'And Nathan,' her mother added gently.

'No.'

'Why are you so stubborn, love? How can you doubt his feelings when he's almost made himself ill in his devotion to you these last days, refusing to leave your side?'

Annie shook her head, the tears finally breaking free. 'You don't understand. He's a dedicated doctor and he probably felt obligated.'

'What nonsense!'

'You don't know what I did to him, Mum. He told me it was finished between us. When I go home I know he's going to leave, and it's all my fault. I don't deserve him. I realised too late the mistakes I made and how I really feel about him.'

'Annie, love, don't do this to yourself,' her mother protested, wrapping her arms around her. 'Tell me what you think you've done—what you think I won't understand.'

Allowing herself to be hugged, Annie sobbed out the whole sorry story.

After finishing a shortened stint in A and E, Nathan had a quick shower and changed his clothes in the men's locker room, then made his way up to the ward. However foolish he was being, setting himself up for heartbreak all over again, he couldn't keep away from Annie. He wanted to make the most of whatever time he had left with her, to know she was going to be all right. Despite the fact that she had broken his heart—not once, but twice—he didn't know how he was ever going to walk away...or survive without her in his life.

As he approached her room he heard sobbing and the murmur of voices. Cautiously he peeped through the small window in the door and saw Annie in tears, being held in her mother's arms as Eve spoke gently to her. Part of him wanted to rush in, to know what was wrong, to comfort her. But he held back, knowing he had to distance himself, respecting that maybe it was Eve who Annie needed most right now.

'Are you going or coming?'

Will's voice sounded behind him and Nathan jumped. 'Not sure,' he replied, turning to face the other man and gesturing towards the door.

'Ah,' Will murmured after a quick glance through the window. 'Looks like they need some time.'

'That was my thought.'

'Good. Then now is the perfect moment for us to have that talk,' the man who had become both friend and adversary decreed.

Uneasy, Nathan reluctantly followed Will to the stairs. 'Where are we going?'

'The Strathlochan Arms. You need a good meal after days of neglecting yourself,' he added, understanding mixed with a hint of chiding in his tone. 'We can have a drink and something to eat.'

A short while later they were in the large but homely pub, a favourite haunt of many of the local medical and emergency personnel. Nathan found a table near a roaring log fire and sat down, worrying about what Will was going to say, puzzled anew at the man's friendliness when they were, effectively, rivals for Annie's affections. Or were they? Could Will afford to be so generous because he was secure about his place in Annie's heart?

Before he had time to sort through his troubled thoughts, Will crossed from the bar and set two pints of Guinness on the table.

'The food won't be long.'

'What are we doing here, Will?' he asked, after they had both taken a drink from their glasses.

'Annie could be allowed home tomorrow, and she's going to need someone with her for the foreseeable future. For a start we need to work out a rota,' Will stated, as if he'd given the idea much thought. 'We can make sure we co-ordinate our shifts so one of us is always on hand for her. And I know her friends will want to help, too.'

Nathan rubbed a hand across his jaw, filled with myriad emotions. Predominant amongst them was guilt—guilt that he had made love with Annie, was still in love with her. Will knew the latter—Nathan had told him straight out how he felt about her and why he had come to Strathlochan—but the former...? Despite everything, he liked Will, and he didn't want to be the cause of hurting him.

'Will—'

'Look, Nathan,' he interrupted, a serious expression on his normally jovial face as he dragged the fingers of one hand through his spiky blond hair. 'It's past time we cut to the chase here. There are things you need to know.'

Nathan sucked in a breath and tried to keep calm. 'What things?'

'I love Annie.'

Will's words caused Nathan's heart to plummet as he saw all his hopes and dreams turning to dust, and the prospect of losing Annie once more a stark reality. 'I know,' he murmured, staring into the flickering flames of the nearby fire without seeing anything and remembering his promise to Annie...that he would walk away if she chose Will. How, he didn't know. He *did* know that he would never recover from her.

'I don't think you do. She's my best friend and I'll love her for ever,' Will said now, sincerity evident in his voice. 'But I'm not *in love* with her.' The qualification had Nathan's gaze snapping back in time to see amusement flash in Will's eyes before being replaced by wary uncertainty as he continued, his voice low, 'Annie and I have never been involved that way—we couldn't be, because I'm gay.'

Nathan was in the process of taking a fortifying drink as Will spoke, but the shock of the words he was hearing caused the liquid to go down the wrong way. As he choked, struggling to return his glass safely to the table, Will chuckled and helped by slapping him on the back. His eyes were still watering as their food arrived.

For several moments Nathan forced himself to eat something, but he tasted little of the chicken, leek and broccoli pie. All he could think about was the fact that Annie had been lying to him from the first day he had met up with her again. So had Will. *Why?* He was confused and hurt, but he gave himself time to think, stopping himself from rushing in and saying something he would later regret. He needed to know the full story.

'So how did all this happen?' he asked, pushing his empty plate aside.

'Annie and I started in Strathlochan on the same day. We were assigned to the same consultant, and we hit it off straight away. Our boss turned out to be a dinosaur—very much of the old school, rude to patients, and a bully to his junior staff and the nurses. Thankfully he's long retired now, but he didn't think women should be doctors and he was vocally homophobic. He didn't know I was gay. No one here knew me, so I kept quiet, knowing how much worse it would be if he found out. He made our lives a misery those first few months, and Annie and I gravitated together, giving each other support. I was in a relationship then, with a guy called Carl, and things were rocky. Annie could see I was unhappy. When she encouraged me to talk I took the plunge and confided in her. She was brilliant.

'When Carl and I split up a short while later I had nowhere to live. Annie insisted I move in and share the house with her,' Will explained, pausing a moment to take a drink. 'It worked out perfectly. Neither Annie nor I wanted to get involved with anyone else, so we slipped into being each other's escort to hospital dos, weddings—that kind of thing. I knew her side of the story about her relationship with you—it was raw when Annie and I first met. When you turned up here she panicked. I had no idea what was going on that first day.'

Will shook his head, his smile wry. 'I had an SOS text

to pick her up at the end of her shift. No one was more surprised than me when she flung herself into my arms in front of you and begged me to play along. I was reluctant. We argued about it at home, but I finally agreed to do what she wanted...although only for a day or two, until she decided what to do and talked to you. Once I came to know you, to understand what had really happened, and saw that you still cared about each other, I started trying to talk her round. She can be very stubborn.'

'Tell me about it.' Despite everything, Nathan smiled. He sat for a moment in silence, absorbing what he had learned, examining his feelings, thinking back over the events of the last couple of weeks. A light dawned. 'So Annie set you up with Anthony?'

'Yeah! Not that I'm complaining! We've been seeing each other,' he admitted, his expression making it obvious how happy he was, and to whom he had been referring in the staffroom when he had declared himself in love. With Anthony, not Annie. 'It's time I moved on with my life, took another chance.' He met Nathan's dark gaze. 'And it's time Annie did, too.'

'She's not been dating?'

'I think you need to talk with Annie about all this, but, no, there's been no one since you.'

Nathan couldn't hide his surprise, and a warm glow began to thaw the icy chill inside him at the knowledge that Annie, like himself, hadn't been with anyone else.

He was trying to assimilate all the information and what it might mean to his future...if he had one with Annie after all...when Will began speaking again.

'I don't understand how she blocked out the full truth of what happened between you five years ago, but I honestly think the self-deception was genuine.'

'I came to that conclusion, too.' Nathan sighed, rubbing a hand across his jaw, remembering how hurt and frustration had led him to call Annie on her reaction to what Julia had done to Gus Buchanan—trapping him by getting pregnant without his knowledge or agreement. 'Perhaps I pushed Annie too hard.'

'No. It wasn't your fault, Nathan. She needed to face the past, to acknowledge the truth,' Will reassured him.

'Maybe. But I'm not blameless. There were things I should have told her all those years ago…the reasons why it was the wrong time for us to get married and start a family.'

Will nodded his agreement. 'You can tell her now. You have another chance—don't waste it.'

'Annie's been pulling back the last couple of days, showing signs she doesn't want me around. We had words before she was hurt. I refused to listen to her explanation,' Nathan admitted, seeing from the expression in Will's eyes that he already knew what he was talking about.

'I know. She told me what happened, and I'm not at all surprised you reacted as you did. Anyone would have. But she didn't mean it the way it sounded. She wanted to tell you the truth…even if it meant you could never forgive her.'

'And now she's forgotten all that happened.'

'Which is likely only temporary,' Will reminded him.

Almost sick with nervousness and growing hope, Nathan let down some of his guard and shared his uncertainty with Will who had so unexpectedly become a good friend over the last two weeks. 'You think there's still a chance that Annie *does* feel something for me?'

'The other night would never have happened if she didn't. She wouldn't have been so hung up about you these last five years if she was over you—or got herself in such a panic and handled this whole thing so badly. And it was *your* name she called when she first started coming round,' he pointed out.

Nathan sighed, draining the last of his Guinness. 'She's hurt me, Will. More than once. Lied to me. I'd made up my mind that I had to walk away for both our sakes, and I was going to accept the job I've been offered working for an aid agency in Africa. Then Annie nearly died...'

'Yeah—kind of focuses the mind on what's most important, doesn't it?' the other man murmured with feeling.

'I might be the biggest fool ever, setting myself up for heartache and rejection again, but I love her and I can't live without her.' Nathan huffed out a breath. 'Getting Annie to admit what she feels is another matter entirely. What if she doesn't remember or doesn't want me?'

A slow grin curved Will's mouth. 'She will. She does. But in any case I have a plan.'

'A plan?'

'Let me explain...'

Feeling more confident about things, Nathan leaned back in his chair and listened as Will outlined his idea. It could work. He'd have to open himself up completely...share everything with Annie, expose parts of his life and his inner self as he had never done before...but it would be worth being vulnerable if it meant he could win Annie back and love her for ever.

CHAPTER TEN

THE sun was shining through a gap in the curtains when Annie woke on the morning of her third day at home since being discharged from hospital. She lay still for long moments, knowing that with movement would come pain. Thankfully it would soon be time for her medication...the painkillers that were making things bearable and the anti-biotics that had so far prevented any infection.

She was delighted to be home, but she was so tired all the time and as weak as a kitten. Her whole experience in hospital had given her new insight into what it must be like for her patients, and, however kind the staff caring for her had been, she much preferred her usual role as doctor. Gingerly she attempted to move one limb at a time, but she drew in a sharp intake of breath as pain lanced through her. She really needed to use the bathroom, which meant she was going to have to swallow her pride and accept help—something she found very difficult.

Her mother had stayed on for one more day after their heart-to-heart that last night in hospital. Thinking about her tears and loss of control made Annie groan. Confessing how stupid she had been and how badly she had treated Nathan had been horrible, but her mother had been wonderfully understanding, non-judgemental and generous with her advice. Now her mother had gone home to Yorkshire, and Annie's resolve to face Nathan and lay her mistakes, the truth and her feelings on the line had wavered…along with her courage.

Not that she had seen him since she had left the hospital. Anxiously she chewed her lower lip. Before her mother had gone home Annie had heard her and Will whispering together when they had thought she was asleep. The news that Nathan had been offered a job in Africa had shocked her rigid. So he *was* leaving. Her insecurities and deception had cost her the only man she had ever loved—ever would love. The knowledge had preyed on her mind ever since.

Will had been at home yesterday, fussing over her like a clucking hen, making sure she gradually increased her movements and that she did her deep breathing and coughing exercises three or four times a day to keep her lungs clear, even though it hurt. Everything hurt physically. And she had mental hurts, too. Namely Nathan. Will hadn't mentioned him…and neither had she. But she had wanted to—had wanted to know if he had said anything, if he planned to visit her, to ask if he had already left Strathlochan.

A very different kind of pain lodged inside her. What if she never saw him again? Closing her eyes, wishing she wasn't so ridiculously tearful at the moment, she tried to think of other things. Like her need for the bathroom and her next dose of pills.

'Will? Are you there?' Annie called, one arm across her midriff to brace herself against the pain. 'Will?'

She heard footsteps approaching along the upstairs landing and shifted cautiously, so she could look towards the open door of her bedroom. A gasp of shocked surprise escaped when it wasn't Will who came in but Nathan. Dressed in faded blue jeans and a cream-coloured Aran sweater that accentuated the richness of his dark brown hair and unfathomable eyes, he looked sexy and masculine—something she definitely shouldn't be thinking about.

'Wh-where's Will?' she managed, dragging the duvet up to her chin, feeling ridiculously shy now that her memories of the passionate evening spent in his bed—and the way she had acted afterwards—were far less hazy.

'He's at work.' As he spoke, Nathan walked across to open the curtains, then turned to face her, the light shining through behind him effectively hiding his expression from her. 'It's my turn to sit with you today.'

Myriad emotions and thoughts rampaged inside her. Nathan was here—he hadn't already left Strathlochan. But was he taking his turn out of duty, or because he wanted to be with her? She felt anxious and nervy—horribly aware not only of Nathan himself and the uneasy situation between them, but of the confession she had to make, owning up to her deception. Whether she could also confess her love for him depended on how he reacted to what she had to say...

To her dismay she had been so preoccupied that she had failed to notice Nathan closing the gap between them. Now, as he sat on the side of her bed, she fought the desire his nearness always evoked but which was totally inappropriate...not to mention impossible, given her current condition.

'How are you feeling?'

'OK,' she lied, the husky concern in Nathan's voice filling her with warmth.

The hint of a smile at the corner of his mouth betrayed his disbelief. 'Has the headache gone now?' His fingers whispered over her skin as he brushed her hair back off her forehead.

'Pretty much.' She sucked in a ragged breath and inched away from his disturbing touch. 'It's a lot better.'

'I'm glad. The rest of you will soon be a lot better, too.'

An awkward silence stretched for a few moments. Knowing that however bad she felt, physically and emotionally, there were things she needed to say to clear the air, Annie caught hold of his hand. 'I don't think I ever properly thanked you for saving my life.'

'As if I could do anything else,' he protested, curling his fingers with hers.

Annie hesitated, unsure if he meant because of his professionalism or because he cared about her. Still, she had to stop second guessing everything and do what needed to be done. Thankful that he hadn't pulled away from her, she took strength and courage from his touch, and from the way his thumb stroked softly across the inside of her wrist.

'I understand why you didn't want to listen to me before,' she began, unable to look him in the eye. She took another breath, cursing the tell-tale waver in her voice. 'I've made a lot of mistakes, and there are things I need to tell you.'

'I have things to tell you, too.'

'I see.' Annie bit her lip, worried that one of those things was to confirm he was leaving to work in Africa. 'Nathan—'

A fingertip pressing gently on her lips cut off her words. 'Wait. We have things we need to do first. I've got your antibiotics here. Then we can get you sorted out and see to breakfast and your painkillers, before the district nurse comes to change your dressing. After that we'll get you comfortable and we'll talk.'

'All right,' she agreed, feeling as if she had been granted a stay of execution.

She reluctantly released his hand as he reached out to the

bedside table, shaking the pills into his palm before pouring her a glass of water from the jug there. 'Here we go.'

Trying to hide her wince at the gripping pain through her chest and abdomen, she allowed Nathan to help her, welcoming the arm that slid beneath her shoulders to support her as she sat up, took the pills and swallowed them down with water from the glass he held steady for her. Hating to be dependent on anyone, she nevertheless had no option but to accept assistance to get up. A wash of colour tinged her cheeks as Nathan drew back the duvet and she discovered that the baggy T-shirt she had worn to sleep in—she couldn't bear anything restrictive around her wounds—had ridden high up her legs. It was stupid to feel so shy and embarrassed given all the intimacies they had shared, but she couldn't help her reaction.

He made no comment as she fussed to pull down the hem, and was patience personified as she took her time easing to the edge of the bed and carefully swinging her legs over the side. It was an effort to stand up straight...she still felt as if she had been sawn in half. But Nathan was there to support her, and together they took baby steps towards the bathroom.

'Do you need help here?'

Fighting another blush, Annie shook her head. 'I can manage.' She had to retain *some* dignity.

'If you're sure,' he allowed after a brief pause. 'I'll be just outside. Don't be too proud to ask for help, Annie. I don't want you hurting yourself.'

With the gentle admonition hovering between them, he stepped out of the bathroom and drew the door to. Not closed, she noted. Knowing her strength was limited, she did what was necessary. Once she'd attended to her needs, it took a ridiculous amount of effort to clean her teeth and brush her hair, then she pulled on the change of clothes Will had left out for her...another knee-length T-shirt and a cosy, comfortable, button-through fleecy robe over the top. Hardly alluring or glamorous. She sighed, catching a glimpse of her reflection in the mirror. Not that she should be thinking about how Nathan might view her, or about the lacy lingerie she wouldn't be able to wear for a while yet. Feeling a bit giddy after all the activity, she sat down to catch her breath, knowing she couldn't make it back to the bedroom on her own.

'Nathan?' she called, cursing her weakness.

The bathroom door opened at once and he was by her side, sliding one arm beneath her knees and another around her back, lifting her smoothly into his arms, careful to avoid her sore spots. Annie held on to him as he carried her back to the bedroom, resisting the temptation to rest her head on his shoulder, but relishing these brief moments of closeness, breathing in the familiar scent of him. He set her on top of the bed, plumping up the pillows behind her so she could sit up.

'It's a beautiful day,' Nathan told her as he assured her comfort. 'After a wet, grey January, February has started cold but sunny. And the snowdrops are out.'

Her gaze slid longingly to the window, which afforded a glimpse of the hills. 'Are they?' Aside from the brief moments between car and front door, when Will and her mother had brought her home, she had been cooped up inside for nearly ten days.

'Once the district nurse has been, perhaps you'd like to sit downstairs for a while and enjoy the sunshine and some fresh air?'

'I'd love to.' Such a small pleasure, but the fact that Nathan understood and had suggested it moved her. 'Thank you.'

'No problem. You relax while I go and get your breakfast and your painkillers.'

He bestowed one of his rare but special smiles on her before leaving the room, and it kept her warm and tingly until he returned a short while later. Again he sat close to her on the bed. He set down the tray and her eyes widened at the fare he had brought her…scrambled eggs, soft granary bread, honey, a banana, a glass of fresh fruit smoothie and a covered dish, its contents hidden. She reached out to see what it was, but he moved it out of her reach and tutted.

'No, you don't. That's a surprise for later—if you eat up everything else. You need to build your strength up and regain the weight you've lost.'

Amused, Annie relaxed and started on the eggs. They were light and fluffy and very tasty, stimulating her appetite as nothing else had done since she had woken in hospital so disorientated and sore. Much to her surprise she *did* manage most of the food Nathan had prepared for her. He opened the box he had added to the tray and pressed two of her painkillers out of the foil strip. Annie took them, washing them down with the last of the tangy smoothie.

'I'm stuffed. But that was delicious,' she praised, stifling a yawn, annoyed that the ever-present tiredness was creeping up on her again.

'You won't want anything else, then?'

She frowned at the twinkle in his eye as he began to move the tray away. 'Wait. What about my surprise?'

'I thought you were stuffed,' he teased.

'At least let me see.'

For a moment a look of acute vulnerability appeared on his face, and she held her breath, realising that this was important to him for some reason. Slowly he lifted the lid from the dish. Annie stared at the contents, knowing immediately what he had done. Although none of the local bakeries stocked them, Nathan had somehow found her favourite apple and toffee doughnuts—the special treat he had always bought for her. Tears welled in her eyes. It was one more sign of his kindness and caring, and all she had done was treat him badly.

'Annie?'

His voice sounded rough, uncertain, and she looked up, meeting his gaze. 'Where did you find them?'

'I persuaded the baker to make them for you,' he admitted with an embarrassed smile.

That he'd gone to so much trouble to think of her when she had been so selfish and stupid caused the tears she was trying so hard to contain to spill free.

Nathan cursed, pushing the tray aside as he slid closer and handed her a tissue. 'Don't cry, please. I didn't mean to upset you.'

'You haven't,' she refuted as she wiped her face, amazed he could think that.

'But…'

'I was just surprised. Overwhelmed.' She bit her lip, not sure what to say, wondering how something as simple as doughnuts could hold such significance. 'Nathan—'

The ring of the doorbell interrupted her. Nathan sighed and rose to his feet. 'That will be the district nurse. I'll go and let her in. We'll talk later,' he promised, pausing a moment to trail the fingers of one hand down her cheek before he picked up the tray and left.

Annie had only a few moments to wonder what later would bring before the district nurse bustled into the room.

Nathan stood at the window in Annie's bedroom and looked at the view. He hadn't been in Strathlochan long, but from all he had seen and learned he could understand why Annie had chosen to settle here. She was a country girl at heart, and had felt stifled in a big city. During their years of training in Manchester they had often escaped into the countryside during rare time off. Annie was fond of sport and outdoor activities, and Strathlochan would provide all she needed in that respect. The town was large enough to cater for necessities and comforts, but rural enough for tranquillity and quality of life, surrounded as it was by lochs and hills and forests. With its sense of community, natural beauty and excellent facilities, he could see that Strathlochan was a great place to live and raise a family. A place he could feel at home for the first time in his life…if that home was with Annie…

Nathan turned towards the bed. She had fallen asleep as soon as the district nurse had left. Crossing the room, he sat for a while in a chair beside the bed, just watching her, feeling an ache inside him at her paleness, and hating her discomfort, but grateful that her pain was lessening each day. He couldn't bear to see her hurt. But at least she was alive.

The love he felt for her threatened to swamp him, but despite all he had found out from his talk with Will he still felt uncertain and racked with nerves. Annie was as skittish as a fawn around him, and he was concerned that she didn't care about him and wouldn't be prepared to give him a second chance. If he didn't feel so anxious and unsure of himself her outrageous deception and her plan to keep him at bay using Will as a shield would be funny. He could only hope Will was right, and that her desperation to manufacture a non-existent relationship had been because she still cared about *him*, was scared she'd let him get close again and give in to temptation.

Now he understood their relationship and friendship, he was grateful Annie had had someone as caring and kind as Will in her life. It was just as well he liked the other man. He knew Will would always be a part of Annie's life—of both their lives, if Annie gave him the opportunity to prove to her how much he loved her. But if he hoped to succeed in winning her back he had to do the thing he found most difficult—expose all the raw and hidden places within himself, the part of him nobody knew. He had to open himself up to scrutiny and judgement and possible rejection.

Annie stirred, a frown creasing her brow as she began to move and encountered soreness. Edging closer, Nathan took her hand, stroking her warm, soft skin with his fingers, noting that the bruises from the insertion of the cannulas in her arm and the back of her hand were fading.

'Hello, sleepyhead.'

'Hi.' Sooty lashes parted and slumberous blue eyes focused on him. 'Sorry. I can't seem to stop napping.'

He shook his head, swift to reassure her. 'Your body has been through a huge trauma. It's going to take time. Are you still feeling up to a change of surroundings?' he asked after a moment, knowing they couldn't put off their talk much longer.

'Yes,' she agreed, but the edge to her voice made it clear that Annie was equally aware of what was to come.

It took a few minutes to help her off the bed. Knowing that it was important for her to take short walks, he helped support her as she stepped gingerly across the bedroom and along the corridor. Once at the stairs, however, he wasn't taking any risks, and he insisted on easing her down with the utmost care. On reaching the bottom, he carried her through to the south-facing sun room at the back of the house, where he gently seated her in a comfortable armchair. The room was very warm, but he tucked a rug around her and opened the patio door, so she could enjoy the feel and taste of fresh air as he had promised, thankful that the February day was unseasonably mild.

Sitting in the chair next to her, he knew the time had come. 'Annie—'

'Please,' she said quickly, forestalling him. 'I need to say some things first…things I should have said long ago.'

'All right.'

'I was very wrong five years ago,' Annie told him, rushing ahead before she lost her nerve. 'I didn't realise at the time that I'd been left with so many insecurities after Dad died.'

'I knew how unsettled you were, and grief can have many effects,' Nathan told her, understanding even now, in spite of what she had done to him.

'Yes, but I somehow translated that in my mind to a desperate need for security, convincing myself that I had to get you to commit or I'd lose you too.' She sucked in another breath. 'In the end I did just that, by pushing so selfishly for marriage and a baby.'

Nathan nodded, and the hurt and confusion in his eyes tore at her heart. 'We were both too young, and not ready for that kind of responsibility, Annie. I said not yet—you heard no.'

'I know. And I'm sorry I behaved so badly and hurt you. Sorry, too, that I somehow twisted reality, burying my own culpability and blaming you. A coping mechanism, I suppose. Self-delusion?' she added, trying a self-mocking smile but failing.

'It wasn't all you, Annie,' Nathan announced into the silence.

Clasping her hands in her lap, she looked at him, noting the wary anxiety on his face as he continued talking.

'Some of the blame was mine. If I had talked more about myself in all the time we were together you would have had a better idea of my caution, why I wasn't able to undertake that kind of commitment at that point.'

'What do you mean?'

Annie was all too aware of how remiss she had been in never asking about his background. It had been such a shock when both Nathan and her mother had recently pointed out just how little she really knew about him, and she felt guilty that she had been so negligent, so light-hearted, taking life and Nathan for granted. Hearing his deep sigh, she read his tension, noted the strong angles of his handsome profile as he stared out at the small back garden, where clumps of snowdrops were indeed blooming, with the promise of spring to come.

'Nathan?'

'I was twelve when my father died. He was in construction and he was killed in an accident on site.'

Even though his husky voice was devoid of emotion, and he appeared outwardly calm, Annie could sense that there was turbulence underneath. Almost holding her breath, she waited for him to continue.

'My mother, never strong emotionally or physically, went to pieces. I was the eldest of four children and it fell to me to keep things together. I had to make sure we had clothes to wear and food to eat, that the three younger ones got to school...and I had to care for my mother, who was in poor health and had a drinking problem.'

He paused again, as if gathering himself, and Annie clenched her hands into fists. There had been so much left unsaid, but now she could read between the lines and see the image all too clearly in her mind—a lost childhood, a boy burdened by responsibilities, growing up too fast, shouldering things no one his age should ever have to face. No wonder he was so serious, so alone, so uncomfortable in social settings. He must have missed out on so much...on friendships, and on all the kinds of things a teenager should experience.

'I somehow managed to keep up my own education, and I held on to my dream of being a doctor,' Nathan continued. 'Not that I believed it would happen. I had to stay at home until the others were of age and able to fend more for themselves…that's why I started medical school when I was twenty-two. By then my twin brothers were nineteen and in apprenticeships, and my sister was eighteen and starting at art college.'

'And your mother?' Annie managed, concerned not to push too far and stop him talking.

'She was holding her own. Enough that she could go to day care. My sister was still living at home, and with outside help she could manage at night and weekends.' He flicked her a quick glance and looked away again, too swiftly for her to catch his expression. 'I felt guilty taking up my place at med school, even though it was the closest I could find to home. I popped home often in my time off to check on things,' he added, surprising her again, as she had never noticed, never questioned his absences. 'As much as I loved them, I resented the pressure, the lack of freedom, all I'd missed out on. And I selfishly didn't want to lose my chance to be a doctor.'

Annie was speechless for several seconds. 'How can you possibly consider yourself selfish when you gave everything you had—all your life—for them?' she demanded, almost shaking with anger on his behalf that he had been put in that position, that there had been no help, no other way out for the boy he had been.

'I felt trapped, Annie, and I wanted to be free. Med school was my escape from that life. It was the first time ever that I had been able to do something I wanted that was purely for me. And then I met you.' Annie sensed some of the darkness leave him as he said the words and it humbled her. 'I didn't want to think or talk about home. I didn't want the responsibilities and worries of my family to intrude on either my training or on my relationship with you. You never asked questions about me, and I was so relieved that I let it go, leaving the real Nathan at my family home and becoming your Nathan in our home. I wanted to enjoy you. Us. I thought there would be time enough for explanations and deep discussions.'

'And then I spoiled it all,' she whispered, fighting another threat of tears.

Nathan reached out and took her hand. 'All I had known growing up was the burden of responsibility, others making demands on me, putting everyone else's needs before my own. I loved you, Annie, but the thought of going from one dependent home-life to another, of taking on marriage and children when we'd barely qualified... well, it scared me. The idea of rushing into that kind of commitment was terrifying—but I never wanted us to break up, never wanted you to leave.'

'And I never gave you the chance to explain,' she added, giving up the hopeless task of stemming her tears. Tears for him—the lonely boy and the man so alone. 'I thought you were rejecting me, that you didn't care about me. I behaved so stupidly, Nathan. I'm ashamed at how selfish and immature and foolish I've been. I can't understand how you could ever have put up with me, far less have loved me.'

'You were the joy and colour in my grey, joyless life, Annie. You gave me fun and love and friendship—things I had never really known before,' he told her, the sincerity of his words taking her breath away. 'Your life was so different from mine and you shared it with me—shared your home with me. I envied you your parents, and I loved them for accepting me, making me feel welcome and part of you. You are all I've ever wanted, the only person who has made me happy. You're the most special thing that ever happened to me, but I was scared of committing too soon. Especially when I wasn't totally free.'

Annie's fingers tightened around Nathan's while she wiped her eyes with her free hand. 'You mean because of your mother?'

'Yes,' he allowed, falling quiet again, and a bleakness shadowed his eyes before he looked away from her again.

'What happened?'

'After you left I tried to come after you, but you wouldn't see me or talk to me.' Fresh waves of shame and guilt crashed through her but she kept silent, needing to hear his whole story. 'Your mum was wonderful—I was a bit of a mess,' he admitted, shaking his head, and Annie bit her lip at the thought of all the pain she had caused him. 'I confided in her—a carefully edited version—and she advised me to give you some time. I didn't expect it would be anything like five years. But my mother deteriorated and I ended up having to spend more and more time caring for her. I managed to get placements in hospitals as close to home as I could, but I had to take a year out when she became so ill that she needed me full-time.'

So that was why he'd been held back and had yet to become a specialist registrar, Annie realised, a sick feeling in her stomach as she realised what must have happened to allow Nathan to resume his career. 'How long since you lost her?' she asked softly.

'Nine months. Her liver was too damaged.'

'I'm sorry—that sounds so trite and inadequate.' She cursed herself, wishing she knew how to give back a fraction of the understanding and support Nathan had shown her when her beloved father had died.

Nathan sighed, a wealth of feeling in the small sound. 'It was a kindness to her. She suffered too much. We had a family meeting afterwards and I explained to the twins and my sister that I needed to get away for a while, to focus on myself and my future. We've never been close. I think they resented my move from brother to father-figure.'

'They should appreciate and admire all you gave up and did for them,' she interjected, incensed on his behalf.

'Now they are older I think they are beginning to understand more,' he allowed, ever gracious in excusing the failings of those who had wronged him. 'They are able to stand on their own feet, and I can pursue my own life, but they know I am here if they need me.'

'What did you do?'

'I took a job in London—a six-month stint in A and E to break me back in, plus a few courses to catch up and refresh my skills.' He turned to look at her then, the expression in his eyes raw and compelling. 'But there was something missing. Something I knew I needed to take care of if I ever hoped to move on with my life.'

Annie swallowed, her throat suddenly dry. 'And that was…?'

'You.' The pad of his thumb traced circles on her skin, firing her blood. 'I had to see you. I found out where you were, and that there was a temporary placement here. So I came. And the second I saw you again I knew.'

'Knew what?' she whispered, barely able to force the words out.

'That I still loved you, Annie. I never stopped. I've been miserable without you.'

'Oh, Nathan.' Tears slid down her cheeks. How could he still care about her after all she had done? She couldn't believe she had been given another chance with the only man she had ever loved. She froze, choking on a sob when she realised she still hadn't confessed the extent of her deception since he had come to Strathlochan. 'Nathan, I'm so sorry. I—'

She *what*? Nathan worried as Annie's words snapped off abruptly and she pulled her hand from his. He felt the loss keenly, terrified she was going to say that she no longer felt the same way.

'Sweetheart, what is it? Please don't cry.'

She shook her head as another sob escaped. 'I have to move.'

'OK.' Disappointed, Nathan rose to his feet, ready to help her. 'Are you in pain?' he asked, frowning when she shook her head again. 'Where do you need to go?'

A hint of pink tinged her pale cheeks. 'I need to be closer to you.'

'I think we can manage that.' Relief coursed through him that he hadn't chased her away. Carefully taking her in his arms, he sat down and settled her on his lap, his arms around her, ensuring he wasn't hurting her. 'How's that?'

'Much better. But…'

'But what?' he encouraged, knowing she was still troubled.

'I have to tell you something.' Her words were soft, and her chin was tucked down as she hid from him. 'I've done so many stupid things—many of which I can't even understand myself. Nathan, I lied to you—I've been lying to you ever since I saw you again,' she told him in a rush, and he felt a shiver ripple through her. 'I panicked that first day. I have no idea what was driving me, how I could have shut out the reality of my part in things five years ago, but I just reacted when I saw you. I felt vulnerable and scared and so confused. So I—' She took a shuddering breath and bit her lip. 'I freaked out and I—'

Again she broke off, and Nathan took pity on her. 'You persuaded Will to pretend you were a couple,' he finished for her.

Her head came up, her eyes wide, her perfect, kissable mouth rounded in an 'O' of surprise. 'You know?'

'Will and I had a chat before you left hospital. He told me what had happened…and why.'

'He did?' Her cheeks flushed a becoming pink as he tipped her face up to meet his gaze. 'Will told you everything?'

'Pretty much. But there is one thing I want to know,' he told her, his tension easing now, allowing him to tease her.

'What's that?'

'What does GAG mean?'

Laughter bubbled from within her. 'Gay and gorgeous. And now Will and Anthony are seeing each other, so I did something right.'

'I hope they'll be happy.' Nathan smiled as he kissed her. 'As happy as we're going to be.'

'Are we? Do you think we can?'

Some of his doubts returned. 'Don't you?'

Annie wanted it more than anything else on earth, but… 'How can you forgive me after all I've done?'

'What we had was special, Annie.' Nathan's expression was serious, earnest, as he cradled her against him. 'It's still special. I was scared I'd arrive in Strathlochan and find you married with a bundle of children, just as you'd always wanted.'

'No.' Annie sucked in a shaky breath, laying everything on the line just as he had done, knowing this was too important for anything less. 'I didn't want that with just anyone. I wanted it with you.'

'What about the foot fetish guy?'

'That was Will's idea of a joke,' she confessed with a nervous giggle. 'There's been no one at all since you.'

'Not for me, either.'

She was surprised, but also knew a deep sense of peace and relief at the knowledge. 'And what about now? What about Africa?'

'The job has been offered to me,' he admitted, causing her already sore chest to constrict with fear.

'And are you going to take it?'

He paused a moment, watching her. 'It depends.'

'On what?' she whispered, hardly daring to ask.

'On whether or not I have a reason to stay.' Dark eyes looked deep into hers. His voice dropped, husky and intimate. 'Do I, Annie? Is there anything for me here in Strathlochan?'

Uncertainty held her in its grip as she worried whether what she had to offer him was enough. 'There's me.'

'Sweetheart, you are all I need. All I've ever needed.' One warm palm cupped her cheek and she rubbed herself against him, nearly drowning in the deep dark pools of his eyes that shone with love and hope. 'Bring the light back into my life, Annie. Let me prove to you just how much you mean to me. Marry me. Have a family with me.' Before she could respond he cuddled her closer, and she felt him shudder, heard the emotion lacing his husky voice. 'I nearly lost you…again.'

'Nathan…'

'I love you, Annie. And I always will. I want what I've always wanted. You. For ever. As my wife and the mother of my children.'

'I don't deserve you after all I've put you through.'

'Rubbish,' he admonished.

She gasped in shock as he pulled a small jeweller's box

from the pocket of his jeans and opened it to reveal a platinum ring set with an exquisite sapphire.

'I tried to match the shade of your eyes. I love you, sweetheart. Five years ago the timing was wrong. We both made mistakes, and we've suffered for them. But now we have found each other again. Will you marry me and make me the happiest, luckiest man on earth?'

Tears shimmered on her lashes before trickling down her cheeks. 'I messed up so badly before, and I'm not about to do it again. Yes! Yes, yes, *yes*! I love you, too, Nathan—so very much.'

As she melted into his embrace, losing herself in his erotic kiss, clinging to him as tightly as he clung to her, she gave thanks for second chances, for the resilience of their love, for Nathan's tenacity in not giving up on her. They belonged together. Being in his arms, her body battered and bruised as it was, she felt cherished and protected—as if she had come home. At last. Completely at peace. Whole. It would take a while for her to heal, and longer before she would be able to return to work in the rigours of the A and E department, but she knew Nathan would be by her side every step of the way.

Taking care of her fragile state, Nathan shifted her so he could deepen the kiss. Annie lost herself in the searing passion, longing for the day her body was well enough for them to take it to its inevitable conclusion. For now the kiss sealed their bond, their love, the triumph of overcoming the years lost to them. Ahead lay years of togetherness, and she vowed to spend every day for the rest of their lives proving just how special Nathan was and how much he was loved.

Here in the heart of Strathlochan they would found their own family—one born of trust and hope and a once-in-a-lifetime, for ever kind of love. Nathan was a special doctor, a special friend, a special lover. A man in a million. *Her* man. And she would never let him go again.

MILLS & BOON®
Pure reading pleasure™

MARCH 2009 HARDBACK TITLES

ROMANCE

The Sicilian Boss's Mistress	Penny Jordan
Pregnant with the Billionaire's Baby	Carole Mortimer
The Venadicci Marriage Vengeance	Melanie Milburne
The Ruthless Billionaire's Virgin	Susan Stephens
Capelli's Captive Virgin	Sarah Morgan
Savas' Defiant Mistress	Anne McAllister
The Greek Millionaire's Secret Child	Catherine Spencer
Blackmailed Bride, Innocent Wife	Annie West
Pirate Tycoon, Forbidden Baby	Janette Kenny
Kept by Her Greek Boss	Kathryn Ross
Italian Tycoon, Secret Son	Lucy Gordon
Adopted: Family in a Million	Barbara McMahon
The Billionaire's Baby	Nicola Marsh
Blind-Date Baby	Fiona Harper
Hired: Nanny Bride	Cara Colter
Doorstep Daddy	Shirley Jump
The Baby Doctor's Bride	Jessica Matthews
A Mother For His Twins	Lucy Clark

HISTORICAL

Lord Braybrook's Penniless Bride	Elizabeth Rolls
A Country Miss in Hanover Square	Anne Herries
Chosen for the Marriage Bed	Anne O'Brien

MEDICAL™

The Surgeon She's Been Waiting For	Joanna Neil
The Midwife's New-found Family	Fiona McArthur
The Emergency Doctor Claims His Wife	Margaret McDonagh
The Surgeon's Special Delivery	Fiona Lowe

0209 Gen Std LP

MILLS & BOON®

Pure reading pleasure™

MARCH 2009 LARGE PRINT TITLES

ROMANCE

Ruthlessly Bedded by the Italian Billionaire	Emma Darcy
Mendez's Mistress	Anne Mather
Rafael's Suitable Bride	Cathy Williams
Desert Prince, Defiant Virgin	Kim Lawrence
Wedded in a Whirlwind	Liz Fielding
Blind Date with the Boss	Barbara Hannay
The Tycoon's Christmas Proposal	Jackie Braun
Christmas Wishes, Mistletoe Kisses	Fiona Harper

HISTORICAL

Scandalous Secret, Defiant Bride	Helen Dickson
A Question of Impropriety	Michelle Styles
Conquering Knight, Captive Lady	Anne O'Brien

MEDICAL™

Sheikh Surgeon Claims His Bride	Josie Metcalfe
A Proposal Worth Waiting For	Lilian Darcy
A Doctor, A Nurse: A Little Miracle	Carol Marinelli
Top-Notch Surgeon, Pregnant Nurse	Amy Andrews
A Mother for His Son	Gill Sanderson
The Playboy Doctor's Marriage Proposal	Fiona Lowe

MILLS & BOON®

Pure reading pleasure™

APRIL 2009 HARDBACK TITLES

ROMANCE

The Billionaire's Bride of Convenience	Miranda Lee
Valentino's Love-Child	Lucy Monroe
Ruthless Awakening	Sara Craven
The Italian Count's Defiant Bride	Catherine George
The Multi-Millionaire's Virgin Mistress	Cathy Williams
The Innocent's Dark Seduction	Jennie Lucas
Bedded for Pleasure, Purchased for Pregnancy	Carol Marinelli
The Diakos Baby Scandal	Natalie Rivers
Salzano's Captive Bride	Daphne Clair
The Tuscan Tycoon's Pregnant Housekeeper	Christina Hollis
Outback Heiress, Surprise Proposal	Margaret Way
Honeymoon with the Boss	Jessica Hart
His Princess in the Making	Melissa James
Dream Date with the Millionaire	Melissa McClone
Maid in Montana	Susan Meier
Hired: The Italian's Bride	Donna Alward
The Greek Billionaire's Love-Child	Sarah Morgan
Greek Doctor, Cinderella Bride	Amy Andrews

HISTORICAL

His Reluctant Mistress	Joanna Maitland
The Earl's Forbidden Ward	Bronwyn Scott
The Rake's Inherited Courtesan	Ann Lethbridge

MEDICAL™

The Rebel Surgeon's Proposal	Margaret McDonagh
Temporary Doctor, Surprise Father	Lynne Marshall
Dr Velascos' Unexpected Baby	Dianne Drake
Falling for her Mediterranean Boss	Anne Fraser

MILLS & BOON®

Pure reading pleasure™

APRIL 2009 LARGE PRINT TITLES

ROMANCE

The Greek Tycoon's Disobedient Bride	Lynne Graham
The Venetian's Midnight Mistress	Carole Mortimer
Ruthless Tycoon, Innocent Wife	Helen Brooks
The Sheikh's Wayward Wife	Sandra Marton
The Italian's Christmas Miracle	Lucy Gordon
Cinderella and the Cowboy	Judy Christenberry
His Mistletoe Bride	Cara Colter
Pregnant: Father Wanted	Claire Baxter

HISTORICAL

Miss Winbolt and the Fortune Hunter	Sylvia Andrew
Captain Fawley's Innocent Bride	Annie Burrows
The Rake's Rebellious Lady	Anne Herries

MEDICAL™

A Baby for Eve	Maggie Kingsley
Marrying the Millionaire Doctor	Alison Roberts
His Very Special Bride	Joanna Neil
City Surgeon, Outback Bride	Lucy Clark
A Boss Beyond Compare	Dianne Drake
The Emergency Doctor's Chosen Wife	Molly Evans